Falastin

The Hope of Tomorrow

Ahmed Miqdad

Written by
Ahmed A. Miqdad
Balqis MZ

Cover photo by Irina Naji

ISBN-13:978-1983749094

ISBN-10:1983749095

DEDICATION

Falastin is a novel that mixes the events that happen with the Palestinian as their daily life and events that happened with real people. It describes the beginning of the Israeli occupation as gangs till today. Falastin talks about love story between a Muslim Palestinian man and a Christian Palestinian woman faced with the brutality of the Israeli occupation in killing, firing and confiscating the lands from the original people who have been living in Palestine. Such story developed from the birth of those lovers till death but the events passed through different stages such as birth, invasion, massacres, separation, marriage, smuggling sperm from the prison then death.

The writers have tried to reflect the suffering of the Palestinian people since 1948 till the day we live. They have worked together to show the real image of the last existed occupation in the world in an attempt to gain support and solidarity to the Palestinians who have been suffering day and night from injustice and arrogance of the occupiers.

We dedicate this noble work to the beating heart of Palestine. We also send our thanks to all our families and friends who always show support to finish this work. Our grateful respect and appreciation to our Malaysian friends who never save efforts to edit and give ideas to accomplish this work especially Norazizah AW and Fathiyah S. Ali Bajunid. Last but not least, our heartfelt appreciation to Sarah Strudwick, Farzana Phoenix Khan and Nilo Murphy for their help in publishing this work. We do appreciate the kind support from the great Palestinian Russian artist Irina Naji to provide us with the cover image.

CONTENTS

1 CHILDHOOD

The morning breeze blew from the east, carrying the scents of the trees and flowers from the nearby fields. In the pure sky, the sun shone over the wide, green fields, its rays touching the peaks of the hills and mountains beyond them. The parents of the two families woke up to the sounds of birds chirping on olive trees in their farms. They had to be up early to cultivate and plant their fields with all their needs in the season. They grew vegetables under the old olive trees. They spent most of their time together, sharing and discussing their daily affairs.

They were two Palestinian families living in harmony, despite holding on to different faiths. They respected and loved one another for the sake of Allah. Mohammed and his wife, Aminah, were Muslims, while Joseph and Sarah were Christians.

There is a story behind their close relationship.

Mohammed's father, Ahmad, was like him, knew no other world except his close family and his surroundings. Ahmad's family were outcast from his big family because he refused to marry the girl chosen for him and instead married a girl the family hardly knew. Ahmad then left his village and started a new life with his bride. Initially he worked for the owner of the land Mohammed now owned.

Through his hard work and diligence, the land flourished. More crops were planted and the earnings for the landlord, Jamal, increased. This made Jamal love Ahmad and his wife more, and he took them in as his family later on. Years passed by and Jamal, who survived an epidemic which claimed the lives of the rest of his family, became very ill.

When he felt his time was up, on his deathbed, Jamal sent for Ahmad. He wanted to talk about an important matter. Ahmad came very quickly. He looked very worried and his heart was beating fast when he thought about that important issue. As soon as he entered Jamal's room, he greeted his landlord."Salam, sir," he greeted the old man with much concern. Jamal looked so frail. Such a different sight from the strong man he used to be. He was holding on to a small wooden box that looked like a treasure chest.

Jamal tried to hide his emotions. He didn't want Ahmad to feel sad for him. Gathering enough strength, he whispered,

"Salam and welcome, Ahmad. Please come closer."

"I hope your health is getting better, sir."

Eyes downcast, Jamal wiped away the tears trailing down his cheeks. He looked to Ahmad again, and again touched the chest by his side.

"I sent for you because of this."

At that moment, strange and mixed feelings filled Ahmad, and Jamal continued,

"I feel that my health is getting worse and you know that I don't have any relative left." A quick gasp of air, "I own all these fields..."

"Sir--" Ahmad started to speak but Jamal raised his right hand and stopped him.

"My son, please let me finish," the landlord continued, "you are so kind, polite and generous." Gasping, "You showed hard work and sincerity in my fields as though they are your own." He paused longer to take a couple of deep breaths then added,

"I have decided to give you all these fields. No one deserves it more than you."

A lump rose in Ahmad's throat, not believing what he had just heard. He stood speechless as Jamal's hand fumbled inside the chest. He lifted up a piece of paper and held it to Ahmed,

"This title deed has been prepared for you. All you need to do is just put your signature on it."

Tears welled in Ahmad's eyes as he stepped closer to the bed.

"Don't talk that way, please," he managed in a strained voice.

"You will get better and you will again walk to the fields. InshaaAllah, you will."

"You must do as I say," Jamal insisted, his eyes earnest,

"No one knows when death will come and I want to die peacefully knowing that you are the owner." More gasping, "I need your promise not to sell the lands."

Ahmad swallowed and nodded,

"I promise, sir. But don't think too much about this, please. Just rest and take care of yourself."

That night Jamal had difficulty breathing. Ahmad called for an ambulance to bring Jamal to the hospital. As soon as he reached the emergency unit, he was given the respiratory assistance. When his condition stabilised, he was moved to the normal ward. Ahmad faithfully waited by his side, forsaking his own comfort and ignoring his sleepiness. Reciting the Al Quran whenever he is awake, Ahmad hopes that Jamal would feel tranquil listening to the verses. A male nurse came by to check on Jamal every few hours. He lives nearby Jamal's orchard and knew Ahmad. He gave encouraging words to Ahmad because he saw how devastated Ahmad looked.

Ahmad hardly left Jamal's side, except to do his prayers. Even so, he would ask the male nurse to keep an eye on his landlord while he was gone. Ahmad had come to terms with Jamal's condition and knew he would soon lose him. He needed to make sure Jamal had the best care before meeting his Creator. The kind-hearted man had been more than a landlord to Ahmad. He was a mentor, and at times, more like a father whom he could run to whenever he faced any difficulty during his estranged life. He vowed to give his best support to the old man whom had trusted his land upon him.

Even though Jamal could no longer talk, the doctor assured Ahmad that he could still respond to people talking to him. His eyes showed the emotion when Ahmad spoke to him softly.

"You don't have to worry about anything, Sir. I promise you that I will take good care of the fields for you. I will make sure it flourishes under my care. I will never let them fall to other people's hands. Please Sir, think only of Allah. May Allah make ease your journey back to Him."

Ahmad saw a faint smile from Jamal and a twinkling from his eyes. After guidance from Ahmad, Jamal said his final *shahadah*. Not long after that he shut his eyes forever and Ahmad was left to handle the procedures for his burial. By the time of *azan,* Jamal was prepared to be brought to the nearest masjid for final prayers on him to be conducted and then to the cemetery. After Jamal was buried, a small ritual of reminder for those left behind was conducted by Imam of the masjid. At this point Ahmad was feeling lost and lonely but had come to terms that every living being will taste death. He returned home and opened his house to accept guests. People who knew Jamal came from near and far to offer condolences to Ahmad.

Life continued to be good to Ahmad. He remained friendly and kind to everyone regardless of their faith. He kept good relationship with his neighbours. He firmly believed that all his good deeds would in return help himself in his hour of needs. Allah ensures that. One day, whilst walking home from the orchard, a car which was driven by a reckless young man hit him. The driver simply sped away, leaving Ahmad bleeding on the ground and groaning aloud in pain. His Christian neighbour, Isaac, happened to see the incident while on his way to town. He helped Ahmad into his car and drove straight to the hospital. With Ahmad bleeding profusely, Isaac tried to make it there as fast as he could in his ramshackle car.

Upon reaching the hospital, Ahmad was taken to the emergency unit. Isaac paced back and forth outside, eager to know the condition of his kind neighbour. He prayed hard for Ahmad's well-being. A doctor soon came out and asked for any of Ahmad's family member. After Isaac introduced himself and explained the situation that brought Ahmad to the hospital, the doctor informed that Ahmad had lost a lot of blood and needed transfusion. Without further thought, Isaac volunteered to donate his blood for Ahmad's prompt recovery.

After several hours, Ahmad regained consciousness and Isaac was the first person he saw when he opened his eyes. The doctor then told Ahmad that he owed his life to the quick and selfless action of his neighbour, Isaac.

"Mr. Isaac, I couldn't thank you enough for what you did for me," Ahmad said weakly.

"Don't call me mister, just call me Isaac. We are now brothers; my blood is flowing in your body."

"Yes Isaac. We will always be brothers."

Since that time, these two families became very close.

One sunny day, Mohammed's family started working in their olive orchard while Joseph's family started working in the neighbouring wheat field. Suddenly, Aminah swayed and fell to the ground. The workers quickly alerted Mohammed and at the same time rushed to her side. Mohammed ran over in panic. He lifted her up and hurriedly carried her into the house. He put her on the bed and wiped her face with a damp cloth, calling her names several times.

"What's wrong Aminah?" he asked as soon as she regained consciousness. "Did you forget to eat breakfast just now?"

Aminah shook her head and offered a feeble smile. "No, it is not that. In shaa Allah, I am going to give you a baby."

Mohammed inhaled sharply. "Are you sure, dear?" Upon looking at her nodding, he hugged her and laughed his heart out.

"Alhamdulillah...I hope this time he will grow well inside you until it is time for him to be delivered. We have to take really good care of you. You won't have another miscarriage, I promise."

The two families were so happy to hear about the long awaited baby. Aminah continued working in the field in spite of her pregnancy. This time she is stronger and more prepared for her pregnancy. After five months, Sarah followed suit, she too got pregnant. They made a big celebration for both mothers-to-be. Even the workers joined them. They all gathered in the field to dance the Palestinian *dabka*, a well-known old dance.

Dabka literally means the stamping of the feet. The stamping however is mostly done not using the heels but instead the tip of the feet. A young man who worked with Isaac started the dance. He acted as the leader and held something like a rosary beads; he held it upright to signal the change of a movement. The song accompanying the dance was usually patriotic and happy. The dancers linked their arms to the next person's shoulder and moved sideways adding a person to the line as they moved. Some movements only required them to hold hands whilst their feet make quick movements, sometimes to the right, sometimes to the left and at times jumping and kicking to the right or left. Sometimes their hands moved up and down too. At one-point Joseph joined in first, followed by Mohammed. Their movements were very energetic and showed how happy they all were. The spectators clapped hands to the tune of the song. Aminah and Sarah really appreciated being celebrated this way. They would remember this for the rest of their lives. They went home feeling happy.

They all worked hard to save money to buy cloth to make clothes and beddings for their babies. Both families were excited over the arrival of the much-awaited new family members.

In due time Aminah gave birth to a hefty baby boy and his father called him Omar. He was a very lovely baby and he smiled a lot. He was gifted with thick black hair and his eyes were the shade of light brown. Exactly five months later, it was Sarah's turn. She delivered a very beautiful baby girl with blue eyes, blonde hair and fair skin. Her father insisted on calling her Juliana. Both mothers dressed them with clothes that carry the Palestinian flag on them. They were like beautiful angels flying in the fields between flowers and trees.

Aminah and Sarah took very good care of their babies. They were glad that Omar and Juliana were both healthy and happy babies. They seldom got sick. Even if there were any signs that a flu was about to hit any of them, traditional medication was given before the symptoms got worse.

With the arrival of Omar and Juliana, both families were ecstatic. The families grew even closer. One day jokingly, Mohammed said to Joseph,

"I have an idea! I hope you will like it too. What if I suggest that Juliana becomes the bride for Omar in the future?"

Joseph laughed. "I was thinking about it too. I wanted to ask if you agree to let Omar marry Juliana when they are of age. Now that we have the same idea, let's drink to a long friendship between our families and much longer if our children marry each other."

They both agreed on that and they drank cups of tea which was prepared on the fire. It was so tasty especially after having a breakfast consisted of home-made cheese, olive oil, thyme and bread.

Then, they returned to their work and each of them told his wife what had been discussed. The wives too were happy with such news knowing their families would be closer still. Every possible moment Aminah and Sarah would gather their children and encourage both of them to play together.

One day, when Sarah visited Aminah as usual, the children were playing together. Sarah said hopefully,

"How nice they look together. I hope they would grow and stay together all their lives. What do you think Aminah?"

Aminah replied with a smile, "Yes, I do agree with you. They suit each other and I hope so".

Omar and Juliana had known one another more than they knew other kids their age. Omar always acted as the big brother to Juliana although they were born only five months apart.

On one occasion, Juliana was running down the hill and fell. Her right knee bled. Omar quickly took off his shirt and tied it over the wound.

"Hold on to my hand, we will walk slowly back to your home," said Omar, extending his hand to Juliana. She nodded and grabbed Omar's hand. He pulled her up and they carefully walked home.

As the kids grew older, they began working in the fields together with their families. Every night, they would gather and share the stories of their ancestors who had lived on and strived their lands with all their might. The children would listen intently to these stories till they fell asleep. In the early morning, they would play with the sand under the trees or ran after the goats. They played. They were very close to each other and the world seemed to revolve just around them. In the afternoon, Omar used to take Juliana to the valley to bring the goats back home. He would catch her hand and walked between the flowers in the fields. To the children, the world seemed to revolve just around them.

The year the children were supposed to go to school marked a new milestone for the two families. It was August and the rays of the sun appeared from the east. Mohammed got up and went to the field to water the olive trees. Aminah came behind him with Omar to help him after she had brought some milk from the goats. They loved drinking this milk daily.

Mohammed asked Omar to take some milk to their neighbour. Omar obeyed his father as always and he went to their neighbour's home. He knocked on the door politely and waited outside till he heard Sarah asking, "Who is knocking the door?"

Omar replied, "It's me, Omar." She opened the door and welcome him. Omar handed her the milk. Sarah thanked and invited him in to play with Juliana. Omar refused and told her that his family was waiting for him. He returned home to drink his share of the milk.

"Why don't you collect some woods to set fire?" his mother asked as soon as Omar finished drinking it.

"Alright, Mother." He went to wash his mug. "What are you going to make for breakfast?"

"Oh, I'm baking fresh bread with a spread of olive oil and thyme on it. There's some white cheese, and I will boil the milk."

Omar grinned, "That's great, Mother. I love the bread, and I'm sure Father will like it too especially when you make it yourself."

Aminah smiled. "I hope so."

Omar left to collect some woods from the nearby fields and took them back to his mother. "I'll go help Father. Let us know when breakfast is ready," he said.

Juliana and her family were at their fields too, irrigating and collecting the vegetables.

Aminah called Sarah to join her prepare the breakfast together., "This year, we are going to enrol Omar into the primary school," she said to her friend.

"When will you go to the school?" Sarah responded.

"We heard that the school will start in September each year. So, I think we must go tomorrow to register."

Sarah smiled. "That's wonderful. We'll go there together then."

An hour later, Aminah took the baked bread out of the clay oven. The aroma of the olive oil and thyme wafted across the fields. The bread, made with love, looked doubly delicious.

Aminah hollered at Omar and Juliana to tell their fathers to join them for breakfast. While eating, Aminah mentioned about having both Omar and Juliana registered at the same school the following day. Since the school was very far, it would be best for them to attend it together. They continued eating, happy over the idea of their children learning to read and write. Even after the men returned to work, Aminah and Sarah still carried on discussing the preparation for school. They decided to make each one of the children a bag and sew them new clothes as well.

They went to the market to buy the materials for the bags and clothing for the children's bags and clothing. Sarah chose a pink piece of cloth for Juliana's bag while Omar chose black for his. He was behaving like a man even when he was still young.

The next morning, Sarah, Aminah and the children went to the next village as there wasn't any school in their village. They walked for nearly forty-five minutes to reach the school. After being informed about the children's registration, the manager welcomed Omar and Juliana and offered them some sweets. School began on the first of September and the teachers would take care of them. Omar and Juliana were thrilled to have met their class teacher, Ibraheem. He offered a kind smile and gave them toys. He added that he wanted them to be excellent in their class.

Aminah asked the teacher, "What lessons are you going to teach in their class?"

He cleared his throat, "Initially we teach only Arabic and mathematics to the first grader. We will add more subjects when the children go to the next stage."

"We'll do our best at home to assist you in their teaching." Sarah promised. "Please make sure that they pay attention to you because they come from a distant village. We hope whatever they learn here is worth the travel the make every day. As parents, we really want them to be well-educated."

Ibraheem smiled, "Oh, they are like my own children and we, at this school, aim to help the villagers to be more educated."

Back at their homes later, Aminah told Sarah that she would start sewing the bag and the clothes for Omar as school would begin in less than a month's time. Sarah, on the other hand, planned to get her relatives in the nearby village to sew Juliana's. She had too much to do in the field for the time being.

"No," Aminah said firmly. " I won't allow you to ask anyone else to do it. I have an old sewing machine but it is still reliable. Let me prepare for our kids' school needs."

Sarah sighed, " I don't want to bother you or tire you. You've been kind enough already."

"Don't worry, please. It is not a bother! In fact, it's my pleasure to do this. Come early tomorrow. I will start sewing the bags first and then the uniforms. Bring Julianna along because I want to take her measurements."

On the first of September, Sarah woke Juliana up and asked her to clean herself and be ready with the new clothes whilst she prepared breakfast. At the same time, Omar got up and asked his mother to prepare him breakfast while he put on his clothes. After breakfast, with his parents' consents, Omar walked over to Juliana's house. He knocked on the door. He had a ready smile when Juliana opened it. She looked fresh and pretty in her new clothes. She too looked him over and offered a bright smile. "Good morning, Omar."

"Good morning to you too." Omar responded.

"How are you today?"

"I am fine. What about you?"

"Fine too. Are you scared to go to school?"

"No, I am not at all scared. I am just excited"

"What do you think we'll do today?"

"Um, we'll listen to the teacher, make friends with other children and I hope we'll get to play some games too."

"I hope we'll have a great time."

"Yeah. Let's go now."

They walked the long roads between the hills and the valley, looking tidy in their new clothes and polite in their manners. Omar held Juliana's hand to protect her from the strangers and the barking dogs in the fields along the way. Juliana felt safe with Omar because he was a brave boy.

When they reached the school, they went to their class and asked their teacher, Ibraheem to let them sit beside each other.

Ibraheem said,

"I forgot your names, would you mind telling me your names, please?"

Omar stood, "My name is Omar Mohammed"

Then Juliana followed suit, "I am Juliana Joseph."

Ibraheem approached her, "Juliana, your name indicates that you are not a Muslim, am I correct?"

"Yes, sir. I am a Palestinian Christian".

Ibraheem clapped his hands.

"You are so welcome. We have many other Christians here. We don't differentiate between a Muslim and a Christian. After all, we're all Palestinians." He paused.

"Today is the first day of school, so we will not study but we will play games inside the class. I hope you will all enjoy yourselves."

After school day ended, Omar and Juliana walked home tired but happy.

"It's an interesting day! The teacher was nice."

Juliana said jokingly,

"Yes, it's nice. But your team lost some games," Juliana teased.

"I will show you how smart I am," Omar smirked.

"I can't wait for tomorrow. I want to learn how to write and count," Omar went on.

"Me too!" Juliana agreed. "I want to learn them too. I can help father count and sell the vegetables and olives then."

They continued talking all the way home. It didn't feel too far then.

The next day, they started their lessons at the school. Mr. Ibraheem was amazed to find Juliana and Omar very intelligent and active students.

At home, Aminah and Sarah motivated them to work and study hard. Once Omar and Juliana had rested enough after school, they began doing their homework before attending to the sheep and goats. They brought along their books together with food and drinks so they could study while doing their chores.

"I think I want to be a teacher," Juliana said one day while on their way to the valley.

"Why do you want to be a teacher?" Omar asked.

"Because it's good being a teacher. I can teach other kids in our village. We don't have a school there."

Omar clapped his hands,

"Yes, that's great. My mother wants me to be a teacher too and I love looking at Mr. Ibraheem teaching us. We will work at our village school together."

After years of such beautiful life between the fields and the valley, they became teenagers and enjoyed going to the valley and sitting down on the rock.

One day, Omar intended to confess his feelings for Juliana. He had been telling himself that Juliana would be his future wife and no barriers would deprive him of her. The following day, they took the goats to feed in the valley. As they sat down on the rocks as usual, Omar became tongue-tied. He was too shy to tell her that he loved her. Juliana sensed that something was going on inside his mind. She insisted to know what was troubling him. Little that she knew she was occupying his mind. Too embarrassed to confess his feelings for her, Omar did the next best thing; scribbled I LOVE YOU on the sand.

Juliana blushed to see those unexpected words. She hastily left him and ran home. That night, she hardly slept, too happy to know Omar loved her. She had the same feelings for him. They later exchanged the love words and messages between each other. They lived a very happy period and planned their future life together.

THE two Palestinian families were enjoying the peaceful life and the beauty of their fields. They did all their best to make the olive trees prosper. They cared for the trees like their own children. Should any of the trees got damaged or died, they would be so sad to the point of crying on them. They owed it to their parents and ancestors who had planted and sweated over the plants with much love and pride all their lives.

During harvesting season, the families and neighbours helped each other to pick the olives. They brought other workers as well because it was the hardest season which need a lot of work. Even the housewives offered their help and support. In spite of the hard season, they enjoyed working in the fields because they could earn money and supply their homes with olives and its oil. The result of their hard work made it all worthwhile.

Omar and Juliana used to take the olives with their donkey from the field to their homes. Omar's father took the olives to the market in the nearby village. He also made olive oil by grinding the olives and keeping it in bottles for the family's consumption. His family used such oil the whole year and they would sell when they have extra. In addition to that, all the neighbours were given fresh olives.

A few years passed by and Omar grew into a fine young man. His father taught him how to cultivate the land, plant the trees from different kinds, and irrigate the field and harvest. He wanted Omar to be able to take care of the field inherited from their ancestors. Since then, Omar became a very strong youth and a skillful farmer. He had earned his father's trust.

During the field work, Julianna and Omar met briefly and managed to exchange smiles between them. They couldn't afford to play around as usual. There simply were too much work to do. Julianna work with the women in cleaning and packing olives. Her mother wanted Juliana to be a girl who knew everything – including how to be a fine wife and mother one day. She taught her how to cook the Palestinian food, clean the home, and feed the cows and also the goat. Juliana became a professional in making white cheese which Omar liked to eat with olive oil.

AHMED MIQDAD

2 INVASION AND WAR

There, on the other side of the world, the officials were conspiring and planning with some gangs in the west, who made a lot of chaos and troubles, to get rid of the original residents and move them to the east. They told the gangs that there is a land without people which was full of blessings – the land of honey and dairy. The great kingdom agreed to provide the gangs with weapons and help them migrate to that land.

The gangs started to bring in youth and train them on how to use the weapons. They sent a number of these brutal gangs to Palestine and made it as their promised land. The great kingdom brought them in as herds of goats via the sea by ships. These gangs came with dirty clothes, hungry, bare feet, and infected with various diseases. They resided in Palestine as poor people and asked help from the Palestinians. Once they had established themselves in the new land, they bit the hands that feed them. They began their series of killings on the original residents. They shot them. They threw explosives at them. They attacked the Palestinian villages, forcing them to leave their homes. They claimed the vacated house as theirs. They acted to their hearts content since no one had stopped them. And no one seemed to care.

Mohammed and Joseph worked on their fields without paying much attention to the happenings in those villages. Although aware about the killings, looting and taking over of possessions by the so-called gangs; they were too engrossed in making their fields as the target too. Never had it occurred in their minds to hand over their sacred lands on a silver platter to the hooligans. Even though some of the other villages knew they would soon be affected, they had no choice. With nowhere else to go, they decided to stay in their homes till the gangs reach them and waited for their fate.

During one of the full-moon night, the moonlight entering the window gave a unique beauty to Mohammed's home. The stars shone brightly as if bringing hope and a beautiful future for the younger generations. Mohammed and his family were in their living room, talking. He looked towards Omar and pride filled his chest. At 17 years of age, his son had become a good, responsible youth whom he could rely upon. Not only that, he had good looks too. Omar had wavy black hair and dark eyebrows with prominent facial features.

"I can't wait to see you married and to play with my grandchildren," Mohammed said. He turned to his wife. "What do you think, Aminah?"

Aminah's face glowed. She almost jumped with joy. The idea had been playing in her mind for quite a while, but she dared not voice it out.

"Oh...that's really wonderful! I too can't wait to be a grandmother, Omar," Aminah turned to her son when she spoke. Mohammed smiled over his wife's reaction. He then said to Omar, I know you love Juliana. I'll ask her hand for you."

Smiling coyly, Omar responded. "Yes, I've always wanted Juliana as my future bride. We've known each other since birth. There's no one else I would want to share my life with." Still glowing, his mother clutched Omar's hand. I've always prayed for you and Juliana to be together. It'll be my happiest moment." Mohammed couldn't help grinning, glad that his good intention had been mutually agreed. "Alhamdulillah. I'll talk to Joseph before we meet his family. I hope they like the idea too."

The next morning, while Mohammed was irrigating the olive trees by the fence, he saw Joseph working on his golden wheat.

"Good morning, my neighbour," he yelled over.

Joseph turned with a smile. "Good morning to you too, neighbour." He wiped his face with cloth around his neck and walked towards the fence. "How's your day?"

"Couldn't be greater! Especially when I have a kind neighbour like you."

Joseph laughed. "Same here. Have you heard any news about the gangs?

"I heard they've reached the village near us, but," Mohammed shrugged, "I don't want to think too much about them. Maybe we can just ignore all the stories and pray we'll not be affected."

Joseph sighed. "Yeah, but I can't help being worried at times. Hopefully the Palestinians fighters could stop them."

Mohammed nodded. "In shaa Allah. Anyway, I have something else to talk about. It's important to us." He looked into Joseph's eyes. "I think it's time to discuss on Omar and Juliana. Can we come over tonight?"

Joseph grinned. "Praise be to God. We won't find a better man and family for Juliana. Please, come. I'll tell Sarah to prepare food for us all."

Mohammed breathed out with great relief. That will be nice. Till tonight then."

They gripped each other's hands and left to continue with their work.

Later in the day, Joseph hurried home, smiling all the way. He couldn't wait to deliver the good news to his family.

"Salam, he greeted as his wife opened the door.

"Salam, my dear husband," Sarah responded with a sweet frown. "Why are you smiling to yourself?"

Joseph's smile widened. "How are you and my young angel, Juliana?"

Sarah poured a glass of water and offered it to her husband. "Praise be to God, we are both fine." She glanced at Juliana, who came to her side before shifting her attention back to Joseph.

"Did you have a good day in the field? You are beaming ear to ear."

"Yes, dear." Joseph sat on the chair at the table. "And I have good news to tell."

Despite the excitement bubbling on his chest, he took his time to drink the water while both his wife and his daughter stood anxious before him.

"What is it?" Sarah pressed on. "Please don't keep us waiting."

Joseph cleared his throat. "Tonight, Mohammed and his family are coming over. They wish to ask for Juliana's hand in marriage to Omar."

Sarah immediately hugged her daughter and kissed the girl's reddened, heated cheeks. "What a lovely news, Juliana. I know you've grown up nicely and now ready to be a wife. You both deserve each other. You do agree, right?"

Juliana's blue eyes sparkled. Her cheeks blushed deeper. "I'll do as you both say, Mama...Baba... In fact, I do love Omar, and he had expressed his love for me since we were younger." She told her parents about the day Omar wrote the three words on the sands. Somehow, her parents were not surprised to hear about it.

Sarah rose to her feet. "We need to get things ready then. Juliana, please help to clean our home and prepare red grapes juice." She then headed to the kitchen to make kunafeh with cheese from the goat's milk. The Palestinian sweet was usually served at weddings, but tonight's special occasion deserved it as well.

Over an hour later, Joseph heard knocks on the door. While Joseph and Sarah went to the door to welcome their guests, Juliana quickly escaped to her room.

Mohammed started giving salutations. "Salam, our neighbours."

In reply, Joseph said, "Salam and welcome to our house."

Sarah began hugging Aminah and Joseph did the same to Mohammed. Then they moved to the living room. The men started their conversation on work matters before the topic shifted to the horrific tragedy befalling the Palestinians in other parts of the nation.

Mohammed continued to say, "This is disturbing news... I will not leave my fields even we all died here. I will stay with you here and we will support one another to face the gangs. Now, let's talk about something else. I believe this news is much better than t with the intention he first."

Mohammed, quickly collected his composure, tried to gather the most appropriate words. "As you know, we are here tonight with the intention of making our families much closer. That is to continue the good relationship we've had all these years." He glanced at Joseph. "This is about what we talked in the fields this morning. We come with honour to ask for your daughter's hand in marriage to my son, Omar. Joseph reached out and hugged Mohammed first and after that Omar. "It's also our honour and pleasure to have Omar as our son-in-law," he said. "We've talked with Juliana about this and she has agreed." Mohammed raised his hands and uttered a prayer, "O Allah, please bless this marriage."

Everyone said Amen to the prayer and rose to their feet. Omar hugged his father and father-in-law-to-be before kissing his mother's hand and forehead. Sarah then called Juliana out, and Omar waited with his heart beating fast. The girl of his dream would soon become his wife. As Juliana timidly made her way to greet her new family, Omar held his breath. She looked lovelier than ever in her printed cotton gown and a shy smile on her thin red lips. Her eyes darted swiftly towards Omar before she approached her parents. The sweets and juice were soon brought out. They enjoyed the meal and continued talking about all the happy things in their life, alternating with singing old Palestinian songs. Now the two lovebirds were officially engaged to be married. It wouldn't be long now.

The next morning, as directed by his father, Omar went to his future-in-laws' field and asked Juliana to pasture their sheep together. While directing the sheep into the valley, they happily talked about their mutual love and future.

Omar and Juliana reached the valley and they sat down on the rocks overlooking the valley watching the sheep and feeling the warmth of the sun.

As Juliana's husband-to-be, Omar was no longer shy to confess his love for her.

"What a nice morning to be with my lovely fiancée."

Juliana flushed. "I am lucky to be yours."

"How did you feel last night? Could you sleep?"

"You know I've been waiting for this day and I couldn't sleep last night because my dream came true."

"I'm so glad too. I thought about you the whole night." Omar Gazed into her eyes and asked, "Do you really love me, Juliana?" She stared back into his. "I've never loved anyone else before you. You showered me with love and tender kindness, and it grows daily like a beautiful flower in my heart."

"I just wanted to hear it from your sweet lips. I t sounded like a musical tone in my heart."

"I do love you forever and ever," Juliana confessed.

Omar caught her hands. "I love you too. I will never leave you."

"Omar, when we are married and have a child, I want both our families to take care of the baby. He deserves to be loved by both my parents as well as yours."

"Yes dear, that should be the way. After all we are all Palestinians."

And the continued making plans for their future. Too engrossed into the conversation, they weren't quick enough to notice a group of men carrying weapons near the mountain behind. Luckily Omar glanced, in time to see the men making a move towards them. They quickly hid between the rocks till the gang changed their course, heading to their families' village instead.

Omar shot to his feet. "Juliana, I have worn our families about these men. You just wait here, okay?"

Panic spread over Juliana's face. "No, Omar!" Please don't leave me alone. I'm so scared. What if they kill you and our families? What will happen to me?"

"Omar became undecided. He worried about their families, but at the same time, had no heart to leave behind his sweetheart. It was frustrating when he couldn't do anything but watched from afar.

The gangs sneaked into the village without any hint of their presence. They slipped unaware through the fields and hid between the olive trees. Several minutes passed before they started firing the bullets towards the families.

Mohammed rushed out and tried to counter attack, but their bullets were faster than his axe. They penetrated his body in several places and he bowed down to his wounds. He fell to the ground and a pool of blood drenched his lifeless body. Upon seeing her husband shot, Aminah screamed in her loudest voice which brought about the neighbouring villagers to the scene. The gangs started a shooting spree on them.

Joseph was shot in the field. He was concentrating on weeding when the shooting began. There wasn't any place else he could hide for the wheat had just been harvested thus making him visible from afar. At home, Sarah was just about to take some flour to make bread when the gunman crashed through the door. She was so shocked that she didn't move a muscle. Seeing her stunning beauty, with clear blue eyes and wavy blond hair, the hooligan decided to have fun with her. Her was about to caress her bosom when another came and shot point blank at Sarah's head. They then argued for a while before their leader ordered them to confiscate the owner's belongings and blow up the houses. They, then left. Leaving behind martyrs piling on the blood-soaked earth.

Upon seeing the gang moved out of their village, Omar and Juliana crept back there. They forgot about everything else, including their sheep, and just wanted to be with their parents. Anxieties and fear filled their minds and spread through their limbs. They needed to see for themselves what happened to their families after hearing all the loud noise from the village. When they almost reached the compound, Omar told Juliana to stay in hiding while he quietly approached his house or rather what was left of it.

Juliana watched as Omar moved with caution. The gangs could still be around, so she prayed for his safety. When Omar suddenly dropped to his knees and bent to kiss a bloodied figure on the ground, Juliana cupped her mouth to control her sobs.

Omar gathered all his strength and pulled himself up. He ran towards his home to find his mother dead too. Both sad and angry tears rolling down his face as he called out to his parents. He couldn't believe they were both dead. He then hurried to check on Juliana' parents. His heart shattered when he couldn't find his future parents-in-law anywhere. He frantically ran to the fields searching for them. Towards the end of the field he heard a deep and low voice asking for help. He saw Joseph lying helpless on the ground; his skin turned blue and his clothes, blood-drenched. Eyes barely opened, he reached out to Omar.

Omar bent over him. "Oh, my father-in-law, how could they do this to us?"

Joseph made an effort to speak. "Yes…my…son. Our… ancestors… died…for…this…land and… now…my turn."

Fresh tears consumed Omar. "Don't! Please don't say that. You will be fine."

"please…don't bother… yourself…with me." With a very strained voice, he continued, "Please…take…good…care of…Juliana…never leave her…" Omar clutched the weak fingers. "I promise, Father." The cold fingers fell lifeless and Joseph let out his last breath.

Seeing he couldn't find Juliana's mother anywhere else he went back to the house. He knew she must be in the house when they blew it up. He couldn't enter the house because the fire was still raging. When he went to what used to be the kitchen, he saw a glimpse of ashen covered hair from amongst the rubble and knew there was no hope of finding her alive.

Omar hurried back to Juliana and reported to her what he saw. She cried out her grief but Omar quickly covered her mouth, unsure whether they were safe from the hooligans. Juliana was so overwhelmed and fell unconscious to the ground. When she later, came about, she still couldn't bring herself to believe Omar's words and about the sudden death of the parents. She needed to return home. She needed to see their dead bodies with her own eyes and say farewell to them. She broke free from Omar's hold and tried to run away but he quickly caught her.

"Please, I can't afford to lose you too!" he stressed. "If you go back there, they'll kill you and I'll be all alone for the rest of my life. Let's get away from here."

Juliana tried to absorb the whole situation and agreed to get away from their village. They went to the valley and hid in the mountain's cave till the next morning. Initially Juliana was reluctant to enter the dark cave.

"Come on, Juliana. Let's go in." Omar coaxed the love of his life in. He pretended to be the bravest man but deep inside, he was just as shaken.

"No, Omar...I'm scared." Juliana crossed her arms in fear. "What if there are snakes or other dangerous creatures in there?"

"Allah be with us, dear. Nothing can harm us. If we stay outside, we could be found and get killed. So, it's better to seek refuge in this cave for tonight. Don't be afraid! I'm with you. I'll go in first, then you follow closely, ok?" As Juliana relented, he began, "In the name of Allah the most Beneficent, the most Merciful," and stepped into the cave. Omar told Juliana about how the Prophet Muhammad, peace be upon him, got his first revelation in a cave, Hira'. They should never be afraid, even of the dark, for Allah would always be with them. They stayed inside all night. Juliana slept with the knowledge that she would be safe whenever Omar was by her side. Omar on the other hand, remained awake all night except for several minutes when sleepiness overtook his guard.

To Juliana, Omar had been truly courageous. Not only did he convince her to spend the night in total darkness, but also wiped away her tears and promised not to ever leave her alone. He would be her father, her brother and her friend. But most importantly, he would be her husband. They shared great love for each other. Other than distant relatives, they both had no one else in their lives. And Juliana trusted Omar with hers.

It was dawn when they woke up and the darkness still covered the place. They got ready to leave for another village where Juliana had some distant relatives living there. Omar took her hand and they started the journey with much care on their surroundings. After a few kilometres, Juliana legs could no longer take her. She tugged at Omar's hand when he kept going.

"Omar! I can't walk anymore. Please, can we rest here?"

"Alright, my dear. I know you're tired and hungry. We'll stop for a while."

Omar looked around for fruits or anything that can be eaten while Juliana rested. He found a mulberry tree not far from where they stopped. He looked up and saw ripened fruits way up. With ease, he climbed the branches and picked enough fruits for his love. He put in his shirt, tied to make it safe for climbing down. He was smiling to Juliana when he came back. "Here, take these mulberries and eat. It will help give you some energy to walk later."

"You must eat too, Omar. It's not fair to give them all to me. We walked equal distance, so, let's share whatever we have." Touched by Juliana's words, Omar took the fruit she offered and ate them.

They walked for two days, all tired and hungry, till they reached a valley. After quenching their thirst at a small pond, Omar went looking around for a container so that they could bring along some water for their next journey. He found one, discarded by some other traveller perhaps. The sun had just set, and all villagers were in their homes. They were afraid of the gangs who would attack the village anytime. Juliana guided Omar to her relative's house without trouble. Despite feeling uneasy knocking on the door at night, they had no other choice after the long journey.

"Uncle Benjamin, please open the door," called Juliana as she knocked."

"Who is it?" A male voice asked from inside.

"Promptly, Juliana answered. "It's me, Juliana daughter of Joseph, your cousin."

Her uncle opened the door and looked really surprised at the sight of a very distraught young lady and an equally dishevelled young man.

"Dear God, Juliana! What has happened? Where are your parents?" His bewildered eyes shifted to Omar, signalling with his head. "And who might he be?"

Juliana fought her oncoming tears, recalling how she had lost her parents and home in a blink of an eye. She forced herself to speak as calmly as she could muster. "We'll tell you in due time, but please can you let us in first?"

Apologising for his manner after recovering from the shock,

Benjamin invited them in and closed the door behind them. "You can never be too careful these days."

Once inside, Juliana related the tragic incident. Concluding her story, she then said, "This is my saviour, Omar, who is also my fiancée."

Benjamin and his family were shocked and very much saddened with the news. They offered their prayers and heartfelt sympathies. Looking at both, Omar and Juliana, Benjamin ordered for food to be brought out.

"Omar, Juliana come, have dinner," he offered.

"Thank you very much," Omar said. "We are really tired and hungry. It's a long way to here, and we didn't have anything to eat except some wild fruits along the way."

Benjamin took a deep breath and spoke in a gentle tone. "I know that my son. What you have been through is tough. I can't even picture how difficult it is to lose our families in a sudden and to forcibly leave our homes. I truly appreciate what you've done for Juliana. To save her from possible death. You have been brave."

Omar blinked back the tears forming in his eyes. "I lost everyone dear to me except Juliana. She is my world now. I'll do all my best to stay beside her all my life. Before I am able to support her myself, I need to find some relatives to live with and get myself earning income. In the meantime, I will have to leave Juliana here. I promise, I will come back for her when I have enough money for our wedding."

Benjamin patted the young man's shoulder. "She is welcome to stay. I ask God to protect and bless you both. Now it's time to get some rest before you continue your quest of looking for your relatives."

"Amen. Thank you for your kindness."

"Good night, my son."

"Good night to you and your family."

They arranged for Juliana to sleep with the girls and Omar with Benjamin's sons. For the first time during the harrowing days, they managed to sleep soundly.

The next day, before taking his leave, Omar said to Benjamin, "I am not breaking my promise to the late Uncle Joseph, but please take care of Juliana for me whilst I look for any living relatives. In shaa Allah I will be back as soon as I can."

"Do you have any relative here?" Benjamin asked.

"I'm not so sure, but my father once mentioned about his relatives in the nearby village. I hope they still live there."

"I hope you'll find them, otherwise, my home is open for you at any time."

"Thank you, sir. I'll try my best."

Omar then turned to Juliana who was already in tears.

"Please don't be sad, my love. I'll come back for you the soonest I can. Let me be able to earn enough to support you. Remember this, my love for you will never fade; no matter what happened to our families. We will be husband and wife soon... Please look forward to that day."

By this time, Juliana was already sobbing away with tears running down her face. Her body shook, thinking about their first separation. All her life there hadn't been a day when she lost sight of Omar. Now she had to go through uncertain period of time without seeing him. She couldn't bear the thought of losing him too.

Omar braved through the teary moments and whispered, "Goodbye my love. Till we meet again, please be strong."

He then turned, simply waved back and walked ahead. He left his heart and the love of his life, without looking back. She shouldn't know he was crying for her too.

Omar walked in the streets looking for any of his relatives around there so that he could put up with them. He went to the market in the village and asked about them but all was in vain. He spent his first night in the village's masjid. The people were kind enough to send him food and clothes while he was there. They sympathies with him.

A curious old man asked him what made him stay at the masjid. When Omar related his sad story, the old man suggested him to go to another village. He could find a refuge home there and the owner would take care of him. Omar was quite reluctant to move to another village and leave behind his fiancée. He would think about with a clear mind when he woke up the next day. Without much effort, he was already snoring away in a deep sleep.

3 REFUGE

Two days passed by and Omar was hesitant to leave that village because he was so worried about Juliana and afraid that the gangs might attack the village and she might get killed. He decided to look for his relatives for the last time.

He woke up early and left the masjid. He went to the market for the last time to enquire about his relatives in this village. He continued searching till noon. He walked from one street to another, knocking on stranger's door asking the same question. He searched everywhere but in vain. He was soon tired and returned to the masjid to get some rest. Thoroughly worn-out, that he didn't realise he had slept for hours; until evening. He was awakened by a sudden jolt. He opened his eyes and saw the old man sitting beside him. "Son, wake up. Have you done your prayers?" asked the old man showing his concerned.

"What is the time now?" Omar sat up hurriedly.

The old man replied, not in numbers, "Go take ablution quickly. You have little time left."

When he saw that Omar had finished his prayer, the old man moved towards him. He smiled. "You looked very tired from searching for your relatives today. Have you eaten anything?"

"Yes, I had some fruits from the market. Alhamdulillah, a kind man saw me rummaging through the basket of spoilt fruits and gave me a few good ones, instead. I went to every street and knocked at every door; I even went to public places asking about any of my living relative but no one seemed to know any of them. Either they have moved away or died. I wish I could meet at least one of them"

"I hope so too"

Omar sighed. "I don't think I'll ever find them."

"I'm sorry then. I told you about the refuge home in the nearby village and it is suitable place to stay in. What have you decided?"

Omar took a moment before answering, "I think I'd better go there and live with people like me. I could make a living there and come back for my fiancée when I can support her."

"You can stay here if you like, but I'm afraid that the gangs might attack our village and all of us could get killed then."

Omar clasped the old man's hand. "Thank you for your offer and advice. I will leave tomorrow morning."

Soon after, he went to a corner in the masjid and put his weak body on the floor. He started thinking about the place. There, he would be safe living with other refugees. Furthermore, he wouldn't have to worry about food. Omar decided to sleep early to be able to walk all the distance to reach the refuge home.

It was time for dawn prayer and darkness still covered the village when Omar opened his eyes. After performing his prayer, he asked Allah to guide him to the right path and make it easy for him. He gathered his minor luggage in a case made of cloth and stepped out through the Masjid's gate. The dogs barked at him as he walked alone in the streets. He decided to walk the way where the trees and mountains could hide him from the gangs. All the time Omar was thinking of Juliana and of his promise to her father not to leave her.

Although he felt guilty leaving Juliana, he had no choice for he, himself had no means of providing food and shelter for her.

"Don't worry Juliana, I will be back for you when the right time comes. As for now, I know you're safe and protected in the hands of your relatives," Omar reminded himself as he walked along.

The first day of his journey was exhausting; having neither food nor drink with him. He walked through a valley and then decided to rest in a cave for the night.

The next day, Omar got up at the first light of dawn and quietly walked till he reached across another valley and started walking along that valley to his destination. Thirst and hunger had become a part of him over the many hours of walk. Loneliness bit at his soul thinking of the family he lost. He cried over and over again. The unbearable scenes of his parents' death kept playing in his mind. He was now alone and homeless. The thought of Juliana and his promise to her dying father restored his strength to keep on going. After a few more hours, he finally reached the village. He would ask the people there about the refugee home.

It was after sunset, and Omar was drained out of energy. He

approached a group of men sitting around a fire. He heard them talking intently about the barbaric behaviours of the gangs who killed the innocent children and people, destroyed their homes, and revoke the use of the land and fields. "Salam." Omar politely greeted them.

"Salam," they replied.

"What is your name?" one of them asked.

"My name is Omar."

"Boy, you looked like you have done quite a bit of travelling," another one remarked. "Where are you from son? I haven't seen you around before," asked one of the men.

"Yes, I came from afar and I'm looking for the refugee home which the caretaker is called Uncle Sami. I heard he still takes on refugees caused by the hooligans," replied Omar.

"Oh! That's not far from here. You walk till the end of this street and then across it you'll find a big house with a large lawn in front of it, and a row of trees bearing beautiful flowers," said the man the first questioned him, "before we go, sit down and drink a cup of tea. We have just made it on the fire".

Omar swallowed through dry throat. He couldn't be more eager to have tea. "O yes, please that's very kind of you. I haven't had any food for the past two days."

"Oh, poor you. Here's the tea. I will ask my wife to prepare some food for you. My house is just over there."

"Thank you again. That's really generous of you, sir". Omar clasped the mug and slowly sipped from it. The hot tea had never tasted that nice.

The man head back home. Several minutes later, he returned with a piece of bread and some olive oil to dip. Omar thanked him again. This simple food never seemed to be more delicious than at that moment.

"Go slow boy. You will choke if you continue eating that way," the kind man said. After letting Omar eat in peace for a while, he added, "So, what is your story?"

Omar paused, drained the tea and began, "It's a very long and miserable story… I've just been made orphaned and homeless. I lost everything to those barbarians. Alhamdulillah my fiancée and I were spared because we were in the fields some distance away, looking after the goats grazing, when they went crazy and killed everyone there." Omar poured out the whole story on how the attack took away everything dear to him—his family, Juliana's family, the neighbours, their homes and the cherished lands. "…I have no choice but to leave my fiancée with her relatives and look for a refuge home now."

Just then another man stood up and said,

"Come…follow me, I will bring you to the house. I know Sami well."

"Thank you, sir, I really appreciate your help," Omar said gratefully. Before making a move, Omar thanked the man who gave him food and drink.

The man who offered to take Omar came over and extended his hand.

"My name is Bassam," he said, "it is very unfortunate that you have to endure such hardship at such a young age. I hope you will find solace at Sami's home".

Omar accepted Bassam's hand.

"Yes sir, I hope to be able to do something worthy while being there and later fetch my fiancée so that we can proceed with the wedding in due time."

Omar was glad he found friendly and helpful people along his way to the home.

When they reached the gate of the refuge home, Bassam went ahead and knocked on the door of the house.

"Who is knocking on the door? It is already night time," came a harsh voice from within the house.

"It is me Bassam, I have someone here with me. Please open the door now."

Then only did the owner Sami, opened the door. He had to be careful these days. The gangs used many tactics to gain houses. As his house was big and spacious it could become a most likely target.

"Welcome, Bassam." Sami said after they exchanged hugs and kisses the traditional way.

"Welcome, Sami."

"Come on in. What brings you to my house tonight?

"Thank you, I bring you Omar here. He came from a village very far from here. He was asking about a refuge home." Sami glanced at Omar. He can see that this boy had gone through a lot.

"What is wrong with him?" he asked Bassam

"The gangs destroyed his home and killed his family. He has no home now."

"That is indeed very sad. Come on in, my son. You are welcome to stay. We'll talk more tomorrow."

Once inside, Omar found the house quiet. He did not expect an orphanage to be that quiet. Apparently, all the other occupants had gone to sleep.

"I am sure you are very tired, my son. Go clean yourself up while I prepare some food. and Then you can retire for the night in that room." Sami indicated the room two doors away. "I will put something comfortable for aching body to rest.

"Oh! By the way, the bathroom is behind the kitchen," Sami added while on his way to the kitchen.

Omar couldn't wait to have a bath after the long, tiring and sweaty journey he endured. He took his time cleaning up. All freshened up, he returned to the lounge where he found his meal, prepared, on the table.

While eating, Omar sat on the chair and reflected on his life so far. He used to be a happy teenager but now he had to endure so much. He still needed to come to terms with the current state of his life. It was hard when one had to lose everything in a blink of an eye. He wondered how Juliana is doing without him? Could she be missing him just as much? He would plan to fetch her as soon as he could.

The minute he put his head on the pillow and body on the soft mattress prepared by Sami, Omar fell into a deep sleep. It felt like one he hadn't had for a long while.

During breakfast, Sami made an announcement to the other refugees.

"While you were all asleep last night, another brother of yours walked in. He will be joining us and staying with us here."

Rasheed, an excited fourteen-year-old boy was excited, asked,

"Where is he now? Can I see him? Is he also the same age as I am?"

Yehya who was two years older than Rasheed, could not contained his excitement too.

"Will he be with us? Will he be comfortable to here?"

Sami smiled looking at his wards.

"Brother Omar is 17 years old. He came from a village very far away. I haven't got the chance to interview him last night because he looked so tired. And I asked him to rest for the night. You can all ask him yourselves afterwards. While I go and wake him up, can someone please get him a drink and something to eat too?"

The youths were all ever willing to help and welcome their new brother.

After Omar had cleansed himself, he joined them at the breakfast table. There were fifteen youths including him; he counted. They each introduced themselves and how old they are.

After the introductions, everyone seemed to be quiet.

"Hmm... looks like I am the oldest here," Omar broke the silence.

As he told his story, beginning from the invasion until last night when he landed at their home, Omar could feel the warm welcome from everyone. They liked him so much and they promised him to be as one family there. He was so happy to hear this coming from their mouths. He promised them the same and he was lucky to be amongst them in the refugee home.

MEANTIME, Juliana was feeling sad being left with her relatives. She looked pale and forlorn. She was crying all the time pining for her family and beloved fiancée. She refused to eat but Benjamin and his family kept on urging her to eat, most of the time. They tried to erase her tears and her sadness. They supported her to be stronger to encounter her future life. She couldn't sleep well at night, always thinking of the gangs coming to kill her. She thought of her beloved and if he would ever come back for her.

Once Benjamin came to his daughters' room to check on them while they were sleeping, he found Juliana still awake with tears were trailing down her cheeks. He went to her, put his hand on her hair and stroked it.

"Juliana, don't you consider us your family and me, like your father?".

Juliana raised her teary eyes. "Of course, you are my second family and you all are so generous and kind to me".

Benjamin frowned. "Then what is wrong my dear? And why are you doing all this to yourself?".

"I can't control myself. The image of my family still lingers in my mind and I am also thinking about Omar, wondering if he is still alive or not."

"My dear, I understand how you feel and what you are going through, but you will hurt yourself by crying and not eating well. Please promise me to stop crying and be strong to live your life normally. Omar wouldn't want you to do this to yourself. What if he comes back and see you sick, he will think that we didn't take good care of you."

His words made Juliana stop and think for a while. There was truth in what her Uncle Benjamin said. Yes. I have to change for Omar's sake.

She then said aloud, "OK, I'll try my best."

"Good." Her uncle gave a big smile.

"Now, sleep and get some rest."

"Good night."

"May God protect you. Good night, my dear niece."

After a week at the refuge home, Omar adapted to the life of refugees and the discipline there. He listened to his brothers' life stories of how they became refugees. He shared his heart-breaking story with them while tears filled his eyes. All the youths cried for him and Sami wiped away Omar's tears. He encouraged him to be stronger and to believe that everything would be fine.

Being the eldest, Omar, managed to handle the younger boys. They listened to him and adored him. At times, they played football together at the lawn. There was a lot of laughter amongst them. The younger boys asked Omar to help them with their school work too.

A month later, bad news reached him through a new refugee who came from the village where Juliana stayed with her relatives. The village had been attacked by the gangs. Many people were killed and their homes destroyed. Some of them managed to flee to other villages, away from the gangs. Omar was so upset and worried about Juliana's life.

Omar sought Sami's permission to go look for Juliana and bring her back to the orphanage.

"Please Uncle Sami, let me go and search for Juliana. I hope she is alive and well. And if I find her, please can I bring her here to stay?"

"No, Omar. It is too dangerous. Don't go there. You could get killed. You are my responsibility now."

"But I am responsible for my fiancée. I made a promise to her father."

"What if they find you along the way? They would slaughter you. Your life is worthless to them."

"I'd be very careful uncle. Allah will protect me. Please uncle, allow me to go and look for my fiancée."

At last Sami give in to Omar's pleas.

"Alright then, but promise me that you'll be extra careful. And yes, of course you can bring Juliana here and you will be married here. We will all pray for your safety."

When the other orphans heard that Omar would be leaving, they too, were afraid they might lose their loving brother. Although it was hard for them to let him go, they respected his wishes to find his fiancée.

"We will all perform special prayers for your safety and for you to bring back Sister Juliana. Please brother, be very careful. We don't want to lose you. You are the best big brother we ever have," Yehya said representing the others.

The next day, Omar got up early, quietly left the refuge home and headed Benjamin's village. He walked for several hours till he found a man on a donkey.

"Good morning, Sir".

"Good morning, young man".

"Excuse me, it seems that you are going to the nearest village in this direction."

"Yes, son. Where are you going?"

"To that village too."

"Come along, ride with me."

"O thank you very much. You know the way is long and dangerous. It will take hours and hours to reach. I am also afraid of the gangs."

"Yes, I know the road well. I work in this village and my family lives there. I heard that the gangs attacked the village. I ask Allah to protect my village and save everyone in it.

"Amen, I hope so. I have my future bride living there. I am afraid that they might have killed her."

"Keep faith, my son."

During their journey, they talked most of the time until they reached the entrance to the village.

The man advised Omar to be cautious all the time upon entering the village. The gangs might still be there. Omar left the donkey and crept into the valley. He hid behind the rocks and hills. He looked from afar and saw the old man, he met at the masjid entering the place. So, Omar decided to wait for the right moment to meet that old man. Omar walked between the rubble of the homes, destroyed by the gangs, till he reached the masjid and ran to get inside it. The old man was surprised to see Omar again. He had been worried about the boy's life.

"Salam, sir. Have you heard about Benjamin's family?" Omar instantly asked.

"Oh, the gangs killed many people. Some managed to escape to other village. I heard Benjamin and his family were all dead."

A wave of weakness passed through Omar's body. He almost fainted.

"But..." the old man added, "I also heard that the girl with golden hair managed to flee from the home during the attack."

Omar's heart soared. Some of the strength seeped back into his bones. That must be my Juliana! "Do you know where she ran off to?

The old man shrugged. "Sorry. I have no idea, son."

Feeling devastated, Omar knew he had to return to the refugee home without Juliana. The journey back seemed longer for him. The little amount of energy left inside him drained out. And he began to lose hope about Juliana as well. He couldn't be sure if she was still alive. He started to blame himself for her loss. He blamed himself for her loss. He should have taken her with him to the refugee home. His was lost in thoughts all the way back to the home.

As soon as he entered the home, Omar related to Sami that he had failed to accomplish his mission. Sami hugged him and told him to keep faith and not to give up. She might be the one; the only survivor. Omar went to his room, his vision blurred by fresh tears mourning the loss of his beloved girl. In bed, he shivered with sickness and fatigue – both physically and emotionally.

Omar refused to take any food or medicine. Most of the youths came to his room and showed their love and solidarity to him. They were all brothers and sisters who lived as a family in the home. They cared about him because he was one of them. They prepared food for him and forced him to take his medicine. After a week, Omar returned to his ordinary life with his family in the home. However, when everyone else was asleep, he stared at the ceiling, thinking of Juliana a lot and wondering what was her destiny.

One day, feeling tired after playing with the youths, he decided to sleep early. He went to his room and lay on the bed. He fell asleep and dreamt that Juliana escaped from the gangs and she wanted to meet him soon. His eyes popped open, only to find it was just a dream. He shut his wet eyes once again and wished for another dream of his sweet girl.

In the morning, after he had his breakfast, Omar confided to Sami about his dream.

"Can you describe her to me?" Sami said.

"Sure." An image of Juliana materialised in Omar's mind. "She is as lovely as a princess. She has clear blue eyes with golden curly hair".

Sami looked intently at Omar before saying, "Last night, while you were asleep, our home received another guest. She has clear blue eyes with curly golden hair, just as you described."

A splinter of hope arose in Omar's heart. Please O Allah! Let she be Juliana.

"And her story sounded similar to what you have shared with us," Sami continued in a slightly excited tone. "She did say her name but I was digesting her story and feeling pity for her so much that I've forgotten it."

"Really?" Omar's heart was beating mad. His hopes soared.

"Please, can I see her?"

Sami responded with a smile, "Let's go and see her."

Reaching her room, Sami knocked on the door.

"Salam. Open the door. Please. There's someone here to see you urgently."

The girl opened the door. Her blue eyes rounded on Omar before the lids fluttered and her body swayed.

"Juliana—" Omar's arms shot out and caught the frail body before it hit the floor. He carried her to the bed and waited by her side till she regained consciousness. He was ecstatic beyond words knowing his beloved fiancée was still alive.

4 IMPRISONMENT

To Omar, life at the refuge home had been more meaningful since the arrival of the love of his life, Juliana. Since then, he promised to himself to work hard so they could move out and have their own home. So far, he only had several temporary jobs, running errands for the elders in the village and doing odd jobs for a school.

Juliana on the other hand, had been a great help to Sami in managing their shared home. She cooked delicious meals for them and she monitored the housekeeping chores done by the younger wards. They really appreciated her presence.

One night, Sami called both Omar and Juliana. He surveyed them for a moment before asking,

"Omar and Juliana; do you know why I asked to see you both tonight?"

Omar and Juliana glanced at one another,

"No idea, Uncle Sami," Omar said, "Did we do anything wrong to upset you?"

"No, no, of course not. Both of you have been a great help to me and I really appreciate that."

"All praises be to Allah," Omar said with a relief, "but what is it that's on your mind, Uncle?"

"Well, it is kind of hard for me to say this, but I have to, anyway. The neighbours have advised me to hasten your marriage. It is not proper that both of you live here in close proximity but without the legal binding." Sami carefully explained.

Omar and Juliana exchanged glances again. "Aha... I see. You're right of course. What's your advice then?" Omar spoke for them both.

"Since you've not saved enough for the proper marriage, I would suggest you both do the compulsory marriage contract first. I can be

Juliana's representative."

Omar turned and gazed at Juliana for a moment. Her glowing face and the shy smile on her lips gave him the needed answer. Still he posed the question. "What do you think, Juliana?"

She returned his gaze with stars in her eyes. "Omar, I've been waiting to be your wife all my life. We couldn't make it happen before—" She swallowed and blinked back the oncoming tears. "I think... we'll do as Uncle suggests, for now."

Omar blinked back his own tears too. He wished he could simply hug her.

Sami smiled. "That's good then. Still, you two must abide by the law and should not live together until the marriage celebration is properly done."

The home arranged a small party to celebrate the commencement of exchanged vows between Omar and Sami, as the representative for Juliana. It is also called aqad. Sami invited several close neighbours to witness the marriage contract. They happily accepted the invitation to participate in the party. Sami fetched the Imam at the court. He would write the contract. When they arrived at the home, the boys and girls had the decorations and sweets all prepared, the neighbours, all waiting. And the soon-to-be-wedded all ready.

The Imam sat down and started finalising the marriage contract, he asked

"Who are the bride and the groom?" he then asked.

Omar stood up and cleared his throat, "I'm Omar the groom and Juliana is the bride", while pointing at his lovely bride.

"Come here and sit down my son, now where is the bride's father?"

Omar glanced at Juliana, appalled to see tears trailing down her cheeks.

The Imam noted that too. He frowned.

"Why are you crying my daughter, don't you want to married to this young man? Is anyone forcing you?"

Juliana lifted her glazed eyes, startled by the question. "No! I'm not forced into this marriage. I do it willingly. It's just that my father is not here to give me away. He was killed by the gangs several months ago. I owe it to Uncle Sami for his willingness to represent me."

Sadness engulfed everyone present upon hearing her words.

Sami then spoke in calm voice, "I'm honoured to able to act on your father's behalf, after all, you're my responsibility in this home."

"Of course," Juliana smiled to him, "you are like a father to me now."

The Imam tried to break the silent atmosphere by clearing his throat,

"That settled, then. Let's continue with what we intend to do here.

Sami, come closer and join hands with Omar. Please repeat after me … "

After the Imam had finished the contract, Sami and Omar hugged each other. Everyone congratulated Omar and Juliana and wished them a happy life away from sadness and troubles.

The happy ambience at the refugee home continued as the occupants started celebrating and distributing sweets. The youths danced the Palestinian dabka and the girls clapped them on to support the youths. The party continued till late night, before Sami advised them to go to sleep.

Soon after the others left, Omar asked Juliana to join him in the garden.

As they walked, Omar inhaled the sweet scent of flowers. It helped calm his anxious heart. He caught his wife's hand and could almost feel the same tremors running through her. The clear moon in the sky looked upon them. The still and dim surrounding embraced them. A new chapter in their life was about to begin.

Omar looked at his wife lovingly, "Juliana, are you as happy as I am right now?"

She gripped his hand holding hers. "I am the happiest girl alive."

"Alhamdulillah, thanks to Allah for today," Omar said. "Now I need to look for a proper job so that we can live on own. I'll work hard in the coming months and hopefully, I'll be able to get a new home for us."

"Yes, I want us to live together more than anything, Omar. I hope you can find work in one of the nearby fields. How about asking Uncle Sami about it?"

"I will ask him tomorrow morning. For now, I am going to miss you in my nights. I wish you sweet dreams, my darling. See you again in the morning. " He bend and dropped a brief kiss on Juliana's cheeks.

Juliana held on to her husband's hand a moment longer before pulling hers away.

"I will miss you too. Sweet dreams my honey."

Omar watched as Juliana headed to the girls' quarters until she was out of sight. He then made his way to the boys' quarters and into his room. He lay in bed thinking about their future and how would destiny help them. He wished he had enough money for the announcement party and a house for them to call home. He can't wait to live together with his bride.

In the morning, after Omar had done his rituals, he decided to approach Sami. He went to Sami's room and knocked on the door. Sami answered and invited him in.

"Good morning, my uncle," Omar greeted.

Sitting on a chair facing the door, Sami replied,

"Welcome, Omar. Good morning."

"How are you today?

"Alhamdulillah. I am fine and happy for you."

"I want to thank you for making it possible for me to be married to Juliana. I am also sorry to bother you at this hour, but you know I am a husband now and have a responsibility for my wife. So now, I want look for a proper job."

"I couldn't agree with you more. You need to start building your own family; but what kind of work are you looking for, young man?"

Without hesitation, Omar answered,

"I have worked in fields before and I will look for a field to work in. Do you know anyone who needs a field worker?"

"That's a good job! I have a friend who owns a big field with olive trees. I will ask him to help you."

Omar was delighted with this news. He earlier hoped that Sami could give a name whom he could go and ask for the job. Now the kind uncle seemed to offer more than Omar had expected.

"That's so kind of you, uncle. I really appreciate all your help."

"Don't worry my son. Keep faith. Now let's go see if there's any food for breakfast."

"God willing. Yes, let's go. I can't wait to see my wife this morning," he said smiling from ear to ear.

Soon after breakfast, Sami left the refugee home. Without saying where he was going, as he usually did, leaving the children wondering of his whereabouts. Even though he knew where the kind uncle had gone to, Omar kept quiet. He was actually praying hard for him to be able to be given a job and a good employer.

Omar waited all day to see if Sami had found work for him. Several hours passed, and when he finally saw Sami entering the gate of the home, Omar rushed out to greet him. After the usual salutation, he said, "I hope you have good news for me."

"Yes, my son. Tomorrow, you can begin your work with my friend Abood, in his orchard nearby. He wanted you to be there before dawn. Please do your best to show that you are a skillful person."

"Alhamdulillah. I am so grateful to you, Uncle Sami. I will prove it to both of you that I deserve to get the job."

After dinner that night, Sami looked for Omar. He was with Juliana in the garden.

"So here you are… I was looking for you in the house."

"I just feel like talking to Juliana here, away from the others. Is there anything you want me to do?"

"Actually no, I just want to remind you to sleep early. You have to wake up early to go to work tomorrow morning."

"Thank you for the reminder. I'll go in now."

"I also want to thank you, Uncle," Juliana chipped in. "Thanks for everything that you've done for us. I will wake Omar up before dawn tomorrow.

Just before dawn, Omar went to meet Abood, his new employer. With a brief instruction, he was assigned to plant more olive tree. He stepped to the field with much zest. When dawn broke, Omar stop to perform his prayers and then continue. The blue sky above promised a fine day ahead and the chirping birds on the branches accompanied him.

Omar worked hard until sunrise before he stopped for breakfast. He collected some woods to boil a cup of tea and brought out the food packed by Juliana.

While Omar was enjoying his bread and thyme, Abood came over.

"Good morning, Omar."

Omar quickly stood. "Good morning, Uncle. Will you join me? Please taste the tea I prepared myself."

"Why not? Abood grinned. "I hope it's delicious. If it is mixed with mint, it will be the best."

Omar smiled in return. "Of course. Here's your cup."

Abood accepted and thanked Omar for it,

"I have seen your work and I like the way you have done it. You seem to have a good experience and skill. When Sami told me that you wanted to work in the fields, I thought that you were just trying your hands at this job. Where did you learn to do the job so well?"

"I worked with my father on our own field. I helped my father since I was a very young boy."

"I see. Then why did you have to come and work here if you have your own field?"

"We used to have it Uncle, but not anymore. I lost everything – my family, home and field to the gangs. Alhamdulillah I managed to escape and find Uncle Sami's home."

"I'm sorry to hear that. Now please consider my fields as yours. Do whatever you think is best to make the field flourished. I trust you will make wise decision. You don't have to get my permission for that."

"Thank you. InshaaAllah you can trust me Uncle, to make your field more productive."

"InshaaAllah. If you work hard you'll be rewarded well."

"Um... Uncle Abood..." Omar hesitated and then went on, "I'm sure Uncle Sami had told you that I'm married. We have yet to live together as I haven't saved enough money for the wedding. We only did the compulsory exchanged of vows in front of the imam."

Abood nodded "Of course. Sami told me you needed to work to save money for your wedding celebration. I will help you as much as I can." He paused and then looked right into Omar's eyes, "Omar, I have been married for a long time but I don't have any children till now... I would really like to consider you as my son. How would you like that?"

Speechless and almost in tears, Omar hugged his employer. "Thank you so much, I would really love that. I lost my own father and now I have gained two great main who treat me like a son in return."

Omar continued his work with inspired energy. How much money he could save for his wedding celebration depended on his productivity. He promised not to let Abood and Sami down, and most importantly he would not let Juliana down.

A month later, Abood informed that he would start building Omar a house at the end of the orchard. Overjoyed with the news, Omar offered to help build it. After work that day, Omar informed Juliana about Abood's plan to build them a house. She almost jumped with joy. While in bed later, Omar sworn to work hard on his house and try to finish it as soon as possible. The next day, Omar was up early and soon he headed to the field. He found Abood had started working on the house. Omar helped by bringing the blocks and the woods to him.

After two weeks of hard labour, the house was completed and ready. The next day, Omar took Juliana to see their house. The moment she saw it, Juliana cried with joy. "Oh, Omar, it's such a wonderful house! Just nice for us to start a family. I'm really grateful to you and Uncle Abood for all your hard work. Thank you so much!"

"I don't mind working hard, as long as we can be together and build our family," Omar said with much pride.

Juliana couldn't stop pacing about the house, walking in and out of the rooms. "See Omar, there are two rooms. Oh, and the kitchen is just great for me to work in! And there is also a built-in bathroom. How apt of you and Uncle Abood. I can't thank both of you enough." All the while Omar look at his wife's reaction. Finally, he gave a chuckled. "I'm so happy you really like our small house. By the way, as for the room, one for us and for our children, later on."

They began to fill the house with the basic necessities—bed, pillows and some kitchen utensils. They decided to hold the party in the coming summer, just a few weeks from now. In the meantime, Juliana moved back and forth between the home and her new house.

One day upon reaching home from the fields, Omar found the occupants and Sami talking about a land demonstration which would be held the following week. They wanted to express their anger and refusal to bow down to the gangs who had occupied their lands and killed innocent people. They all agreed to hold the big demonstration starting from the refugee home and ending up at the occupiers' settlements. Omar informed them that he too, would be joining the demonstration.

A couple of days before the demonstration, Omar went to see Sami and offered his ideas.

"Uncle Sami, what do you think if I write some banners showing that we are against the occupiers. We'll use these banners during the demonstration. We need to let them know that we detest being bullied by the people who acted like hooligans, taking our hands, our homes and killing our people."

"Good idea, Omar! Can you make a couple of big size banners and three smaller?"

"Alright, I will ask some of the boys to help me do them."

With Omar's instruction and guidance, the banners were made ready in time for the demonstration. The male members of the refugee home then gathered at their front gate and waited for the neighbours to join them.

Before the demonstration began, Sami spoke them to lift their spirits.

"My sons, we are protesting against inhuman actions by the occupiers. Don't ever give up our rights to the land we own for generations. If I were to die today, please make prayers for me and my death will not be wasted. This goes for any of you too. You can stay in this house for as long as you like. Feel free to accept more brothers who need a roof above their heads. Our neighbours will not leave you alone. They will take care of your needs.

Remember what we are doing is a small contribution to our forefathers."

The demonstrators soon started walking, carrying the banners and chanting anti-occupiers' slogan. They moved at a steady pace towards the gangs' settlement. Not long after that, the gangsters began shooting on the demonstrators and unfortunately, Sami got hit on his head and fell to the ground. Several youths rushed him to the nearby clinic but the nurse told them that he was already dead, another martyr amongst the Palestinians. Angered, from a peaceful rally, the youths began to throw stones at the gangs. They, in return, started going after the youths.

Omar was so courageous, he was not afraid of death and he was in the front line of the demonstrators. All of a sudden, he fell to the ground, shouting. "My leg...it hurts!"

He was shot in his leg. At the same time, some members of the gang rushed towards the group of demonstrators. The boys ran for their lives and were not able to take Omar home with them as he couldn't run on his injured leg. He was caught, and the gang took him to their settlement.

Sadly, the boys returned home without Omar. When Juliana couldn't find Omar among them, she began asking about him but all kept silent. Thinking Omar could have been killed like Sami. She broke down. She knew the hooligans would not show any mercy on him would likely kill her husband. All their friends were beside her and showered her their solidarity and sympathy.

Juliana rushed to Abood's home to inform about Omar's plight. She knocked on the door and his wife, Rina, opened the door. She gasped seeing Juliana in tears.

"Oh dear, what made you come during the night, Juliana? What happened?"

Still sobbing, Juliana said, "Uncle Sami and… Omar are dead as martyrs."

Rina hurriedly invited her in and woke her husband up. They both listened to Juliana's story. Abood was shocked to hear the news about Sami and Omar. He cried over the loss of such a good young man, who had suffered so much in his teen's life. He grieved over the loss of a very good friend, Sami. Their death, however, would not be in vain. The whole neighbourhood would celebrate their martyrdom. Nevertheless, Abood had a feeling that Omar could still be alive. He then told Juliana that in the morning, he will ask around if anyone knew about Omar. Rina invited Juliana to spend the night in their house as it was already late for her to return home. Juliana agreed. She was so worried, that she didn't sleep a wink and cried the whole night for her husband.

The next morning, Abood went to ask about Omar, but no one knew anything about his fate; whether he was still alive or already dead. He went to the refugee home to see Omar's friends about the location where Omar was shot. One of them began,

"We heard random bullets were being fired at us. I was standing beside Omar when I heard him cry out. His leg was hurt. Right at that time, the gangs came after us and we simply ran for our lives. I saw Omar fell down, but we couldn't rescue him because they were already carrying him away."

Slightly relieved, Abood went back to Juliana to told her what he had heard. There was a big chance that he was still alive.

"Omar was only shot in his leg, so don't worry about him, please. I will gather some elders from the village to go to the settlement and ask for Omar's release."

Abood wasted no time. Right away he went to see the elders as promised. He managed to gather several of them and, together, they headed to the settlement. When they reached its gate, the guard told them to come back the next morning as the leader would only be around the following day. They returned the next morning as asked but again were made to wait outside for a few more hours till the gang's leader arrived. He would decide whether to meet them or not. They waited from eight in the morning till half past one in the afternoon. The leader arrived in his military jeep and instructed them to go to his office. Inside, they enquired about Omar's plight, and whether he was still alive or already dead. The leader informed them that Omar was alive and currently receiving treatment at the military clinic. The elders voiced out their intent to take Omar back with them, but were told that Omar would be detained and later faced a court's trial. The leader obtained Abood's details so he could be contacted in due course. The elders tried to negotiate for Omar's immediate released but were promptly ordered to leave the office.

Abood returned home with a heavy heart, knowing he would disappoint the young girl. He opened the door and saw Juliana sitting on the wooden chair wiping off her tears. She remained silent as if she was absent from this universe.

"Assalamu alaikum," Abood greeted.

Juliana turned to him, replied, "Wa alaikum assalam." Questions filled her sad face.

Abood stepped closer and gently said, "Don't worry my daughter. Omar is not dead. He's being treated now."

Juliana shot up from the chair. "Thank God! Where is he treated?"

"At the military clinic," Abood answered, "He's a prisoner now and they'll hold a court to sentence him."

Tears filled Juliana's eyes again. "I have to be thankful that he is still alive."

Abood agreed, "Yes, we have to be thankful, Juliana. I want you to stay with us in your home that your husband and I have built. I will take care of you as my own daughter".

Abood's sincerity made Juliana weep once again, this time with happiness. She collected herself and said,

"I am most grateful for your offer, uncle. Thank you so much. I am forever thankful to have met many kind people since I became an orphan. May Allah bless all of you."

"Ya rabb," said Abood.

"Uncle, please take me to see Omar." Juliana pleaded. "I can't live without him. We were just about to enjoy marriage and living together and this had to happen. I cannot endure being away from him."

"I promise you that we will go together in the next visit," answered Abood.

Two weeks later, the leader sent news to Abood that they would keep

Omar without a court's sentence because he was always making trouble and creating chaos against them in the prison. Omar's family were allowed to visit him once a month. Abood assigned a lawyer to defend Omar's case and to arrange visitation schedule. The lawyer would tell them any news about Omar. The fifteenth of May was the first visit to Omar. Abood, Rina and Juliana went to the prison to meet Omar. The gangs inspected them before allowing them to see him. The moment Omar saw them, he started crying, making all of them cry as well. Despite being utterly sad, Juliana knew she had to be strong for Omar. She pledged not to ever leave him alone. She would work in the field in order to provide him with all his needs. And if he wanted anything, he could ask for it through the lawyer. The visit lasted fifteen minutes, then the jailer told them to leave.

Juliana informed Abood about her intention to work in the field, replacing Omar because she had the same experience in her own field before. Even though Abood said he could offer anything Omar needed, she insisted to work for him and earn her living. On every visit, Juliana cooked and brought Omar his favourite food and at times, new clothes for him.

"Please do not hesitate to ask if you need anything," she said during one of the visits. "I'll try my best to fulfill your requests."

"Really?" Omar asked in return.

Juliana nodded. "Yes I really mean it."

"Please ask them to release me so that we can live together in our own home."

"You know I don't have the power to do that, my darling. I would if I could. Listen, no matter how long I have to wait for you to be out of here, I will do that. I'll wait for the time when we can be together as we've dreamed to be. Remember that I love you and you're always in my heart and mind."

Her words caused Omar to smile through happy tears. "You know I'll never stop loving you too. I will patiently wait for the day I become a free person again.

After a year in prison, the lawyer informed Juliana that the gangs renewed the administrative detention on Omar. When she questioned him what it means, he explained that Omar would continue to be kept as prisoners without a court sentence on him. She was shocked because there was no specific date for him to be released from prison. Juliana had no choice but to continue her role of a provider for both of them. She had to work in the fields as usual. She also continued to give Omar all the encouragement and support he needed. She told him that he will see the light soon and he will breathe the air of freedom not much longer.

The second year ended and still no news from the lawyer indicating that when Omar would get his freedom. She went to see the lawyer and was again told that Omar's detention had been renewed for the third year. He would do his best to make them release Omar. In the middle of the third year, the lawyer informed Juliana that the gangs held a trial for Omar but unfortunately, they sentenced him with ten years imprisonment. Juliana crumbled to the ground and she cried till she had no more tears. Abood and the lawyer was full of sympathy for her but they advised her to support and encourage Omar to stay strong.

She visited Omar after the court sentence, she told him that Abood and all his friends were proud of him and would support him all the way. She would never give up supporting him; in addition, she would wait till he gets his freedom to have their proper marriage. All her words lifted Omar's spirit and provide him with enough strength to go through his long ordeal. He, in turn, gave his word and never to break his promise to Joseph to take care of her. As for the moment, he could just be content with the weekly visitation allowed by the court for his family.

5 BIRTH OF A BABY

During the years of Omar's imprisonment, the gangs used all kinds of torture. They would tie his hands behind his back. His legs were tied too; and then they beat him severely. They once, put him in solitary confinement for several months of mental torture. The gangs gave him his food and water from under the door. They simply kicked the plate in. They meant to make him feel so low when he had to pick up his food like a dog. The dirty and dark cell had no window; it's size too small that Omar couldn't sleep normally or even extend his legs. He slept sitting down. On top of that, the gang abused him verbally; using foul words to provoke him, but Omar managed to keep his cool. He pretended not to hear anything. Once he almost gave them what they wished for; to get him to revolt and punished him severely after that.

"You stupid Palestinian! Your mother couldn't stand the hardship and ran away to be our leader's mistress. Entertaining him with all he demanded of her! Stupid! Stupid! Stupid boy! What's the use of fighting us? Just be like your mother and live a happy life." They jeered and laughed aloud. The memory of his mother dead in their hands came back to haunt Omar. The gang had purposely tarnished her good self with false accusation. Omar fought to control his anger when she became the subject of their mockery that morning. Consumed with rage, he almost punched the man who and he almost punched the man who spewed those despicable words. Instead he clenched his fist hard, the nails dug into his palm. He finally yelled out and continued with his task as though nothing happened.

The jailers seemed to be breeding all sorts of insects and also rats to add to the prisoners' misery. During solitary confinement, no visitation was allowed. Omar missed seeing Juliana and the news that she brought from the outside world. The only thing that kept him sane was the knowledge that Allah would always be with him and would not let him suffer for long.

After more than five years of Omar's prison sentence, Juliana visited him as usual. Omar saw her from behind the iron bars.

"Juliana dear, it had been too long. I can't take it anymore! I hate everything about this prison. My whole body ache when they hit or kick me. And I get all this treatment just because I'm a Palestinian. And they wouldn't let me get medical treatment after all that. I want to be out there with you. To be a free man and take care of our own country."

As much as she wanted to break down and cry, Juliana controlled herself for the sake of Omar's strength against the oppressors. He must not give in and should continue to persevere. She wanted him to be out of the prison as a man with dignity. And she wanted to live with that man for the rest of her life, bearing and raising his children. She encouraged him to speak out his grievances so he would feel better.

"You're a strong man Omar. I know you can make it. You have protected me in many occasions and I'm so proud of you. You're always my saviour. It's okay to feel as you do, just tell me what other bad treatments you've received in here. We will overcome it together; you and I." Omar then continued, "In winter, I had to endure the cold without clothes. Then, in the hot of summer, they made me wear the special clothes made for mental patients; you know, the one with long sleeves? I was had to wear that and they had it tied behind my back. I was sweating like crazy."

He paused for moments. "Do you know what else irk me the most? The creepy crawlies. You name them, they have it here, cockroaches, spiders, lizards and even rats. Sometimes when I sleep, I was dreaming that you were running your fingers through my hair and I woke astonished that they were actually the rats all over my body! And I wriggle so hard to get the creepy feeling out of my skin. How I wish I could keep on dreaming about you stroking my hair and never to wake up."

"Dear, I don't know whether to cry or to laugh! I can only imagine you wriggling your body like doing a dance; dancing to a very fast music."

Omar's chuckle sounded like music to Juliana's ears. She knew that she had made Omar relaxed. And she knew how important it was to have his spirits high all the time.

Before the visiting hours ended, Juliana added more encouraging words to Omar.

"Please remember that you were put into prison for a just cause.

Everyone outside and especially the youths, look up highly at your sacrifices. They are very proud of you because you are an example of patriotism. It won't be long now; you have served more than half of your prison sentence, you will be out soon. Please keep your spirits high, love" ended Juliana, just before the jailer shouted for her to leave.

Her visits had definitely made Omar more optimistic and strong enough to endure the long years of the prison time.

Juliana later heard of a procedure which enabled wives of inmates to be pregnant whilst their husbands were still in the prison. She made queries about it.

The procedure, called artificial insemination, could only be done at certain fertility clinic. Juliana thought this could possibly make Omar more positive in mind and look forward to his day of freedom; to be able to hold his own child. She couldn't wait to tell Omar about it on her next visit.

On the day of visitation, Juliana could hardly contain her excitement. "I have good news Omar," she said as soon as the jailer moved further away from them.

Omar's face brightened. "Quick, tell me. Do I get out tomorrow?" At Juliana's frown he added,

"Okay, I'm just kidding. Please tell me what news make you beam like this. You had the same look when Uncle Sami suggested that we wed legally first."

"You know what?" Despite herself, Juliana blushed, "Um, I could actually make your life more meaningful and happier in here."

"I don't get you. How or what actually do you intend to do to me behind these bars?"

"I want to have your baby. I'm positive we can do it now. We could do this as a symbol of defeating the jailers."

Taken by surprise with her words, Omar almost shouted,

"What nonsense are you talking about Juliana? You must be kidding!"

"No, I am not. I have a plan and you must listen carefully,"

She told him that she had discussed with a doctor from a nearby fertility clinic about her plan, and he was willing to help them. He would implant Omar's sperm into her womb but the main problem was getting the sperm out of the prison. Still much in shocked, Omar said,

"How can it be done? It is next to impossible, dear. Think carefully, if we get caught, the consequence is unthinkable."

"Listen, I would try to bring a tube for you to put your sperm in—"

Before she could explain further, the jailer came and told them that visiting hours was over.

"Till next visit then," Juliana quickly said to her open-mouthed husband.

Juliana went home and told Abood of her intention to do the procedure. After thinking hard yet still failed to get an idea on how to do it, Juliana fell asleep. While sleeping, she dreamt about making a pocket at the heels of her shoes to smuggle the tube inside it. The next morning Juliana requested Abood to get her a pair of shoe with a thick sole. She explained to him about her plan and he agreed that it could be a good plan. She also asked him to get a tube that could be inserted into the heel pocket. He went to the market and bought the shoes and the tube. With much difficulty, she managed to cut open one of the thick heel, made a hole and hid the tube inside it.

Being a very courageous girl, Juliana was not afraid of the gangs even though they always checked her thoroughly before letting her pass to meet Omar. She anxiously waited for the next visit, keen to carry out her plan against the gangs' injustice.

Omar, on the other hand, had mixed feelings about it. He couldn't help being excited, but at the same time, afraid the jailers might discover their plan and then put Juliana into the prison as well. Anxious for his wife's next visit and of what could possibly would happen to them, Omar prayed all night till he became exhausted. He asked for Allah's Mercy and help in achieving what they intended to do. He recited the verses from the Al Quran to calm his anxiety.

It was Saturday evening when Juliana invited Abood to join her visit to Omar two days later. He and his wife agreed to come with her. They would help her realise her plan.

"Another thing dear, I have to tell the elders and the villagers about your plan. I don't want them to think badly of you once they knew that you are pregnant. I will let them know at the masjid after prayers tonight."

"Thank you so much Uncle. You really take care of me like my own father."

"Your aunt and I were married for a long time and we are not blessed with any child. When Omar came to ask for work, I could see that he is a very responsible young man, caring and a very obedient son. Since that time, I've thought of him as my own son. And now, in his absence, I will take care of you as my own daughter-in-law. Haven't I showed it to you enough?"

Touched by his words, Juliana answered, "Yes Uncle, you have always showed it by being by my side all this while. It is just that I need to let you know how much I appreciate what you are doing for me now, especially for this crazy idea of mine."

Abood smiled and told Juliana to rest well for the night.

At the masjid that night, after the usual congregation, Abood asked permission from the imam to speak.

"Respected imam and the elders of the community and also everyone here, I would like to request that we make duaa for the safety of Juliana and Omar. She has a plan that can defeat the jailers. A doctor at the fertility clinic would do a procedure on her to make her able to conceive Omar's baby."

There were some hushes on the audience in front of him and so he knew what was on their minds.

"Yes, I know what you are thinking, this is almost impossible, but by the Grace and Mercy of Allah, in shaa Allah this plan will be a success. Tomorrow Juliana will try to smuggle in a tube to Omar. Let's all pray that this idea will become a reality."

The next day, they got up early and prepared themselves to go.

Abood again reminded, "Juliana, remember, you must keep calm and never let the jailer suspect anything. Otherwise you will be punished and be sent to the prison too."

Although anxious for what would happen later, Juliana answered,

"I will Uncle Abood. I made this suggestion to Omar and I will make sure that this plan falls through."

As usual, when they reached the prison's gate, the jailer told them to go through the inspection process. Juliana held her breathe and tried to act as normally as possible. When it was over, they were ordered to go in and meet Omar for fifteen minutes. Abood signalled for Juliana to sit down on the only chair. That would make it easier for her to get the tube out of her shoe. He and his wife stood behind her to cover her while she was doing it. Juliana's hand shivered but Abood quietly urged her to be calm and steady until she managed to get the tube out. She waited till the jailer turned his face another way and then slipped the tube through the iron bars to Omar. Omar hid it in his clothes and he asked them to leave. He would pass the tube back to Juliana in the coming visit.

The moment they stepped out of the prison gate, Juliana exhaled a long breath of relief, thankful to God for the successful plan so far. Abood and his wife were greatly relieved too. They congratulated Juliana, and Rina hugged her. They ensured her that the tube would be back in her hand when they see Omar again.

Juliana was counting the days to the next visit and she asked God to make it easy for Omar to put his sperm in the tube. She asked Abood to lend her some money because she needed to wear heavy clothes during the visit. Abood gladly gave her enough to buy them. They then discussed the plan to get the tube out of prison. While Juliana sat on the chair talking to Omar, Abood and Rina would stand close and try to cover them. They would carry out the plan on the coming Monday.

The day arrived, and at seven in the morning, Juliana went to Abood's house. Rina let her in whilst they got ready for the day's mission. At about the same time, Omar asked the jailer to let him take a shower but was refused. After Omar informed that he was suffering from itchy skin, the jailer allowed him to do it in five minutes. Omar went to the bath and thought of his sweet and witty wife until he managed to fill the tube as required. He closed it securely and hid the tube in his clothes before taking a quick shower. He then yelled to the jailer that he had finished. The jailer hit his back and kicked him into the cell for taking longer than five minutes. Omar felt satisfied although he'd had his daily dose of torture so early in the morning. He couldn't wait to see Juliana. Half an hour later, Juliana, Abood and Rina reached the prison and passed through the check point to meet Omar. Omar gave a broad smile and Juliana understood that he had accomplished the mission. She sat down on the chair and Abood and his wife stood close by her side to give cover. He got the tube out of his pocket and passed it to Juliana. She quickly hid it inside the sole of her shoe.

"My darling, you are a brave man. I love you so much," she whispered.

"I love you more, my darling Juliana, I would do anything for you and our country, Palestine."

"Please pray that I will get pregnant soon. If this procedure fails this time, the kind doctor had promised to repeat it for us."

"Of course, I will make fervent prayers for the success."

"I am sorry, dear. I won't be able to come and visit you for the next three weeks as I need to rest and also will be in the clinic to do the pregnancy test."

"It is okay. Take your time dear. I won't be anywhere else but here. I am going to miss you like crazy though, but don't worry. Allah is with us," he smiled dryly.

They, soon left the prison and straight away went to the clinic and there, the doctor was already waiting to do the procedure on Juliana. He was amazed at Juliana's determination and how she managed to get the needed specimen for the operation in such a short time. After going through the usual check-up to make sure she was fit to undergo the operation, Juliana was asked to change her clothes and get ready to go to the operating theatre.

Rina stayed with her at the clinic while Abood went out to get them some food. After an hour, the doctor came out and told Rina that the operation was successful. They would know the result of the procedure in less than a month's time. Juliana needed to rest in the clinic for a couple of days before Abood could take her home. Abood and Rina then, left. Two days later, Abood brought Juliana back to his house. Rina was advised by her husband to take good care of Juliana and made sure she was comfortable. Juliana felt that she was imposing on them and asked to go back to her house. Abood wouldn't hear of it. He told her that she could only go home two weeks after the operation was done.

To Juliana, every single minute she had to go through in the next three weeks was really a test of time. She can almost hear a giant clock going tick-tock in her mind. Full of anticipation and hope, she fervently asked help from the Supreme Power to make her dream come true. She badly wanted Omar's spirit to be high always.

Three weeks after the operation, Abood and Rina took Juliana to see the result. Her heart was pounding so hard that she thought everyone could hear the beats. The doctor took a sample of her blood to be tested for positive pregnancy. He returned with a big smile on his face and congratulated Juliana. She was now pregnant. Juliana hugged Rina and almost danced with joy. They were all delighted and thanked the doctor. He was so happy to make another in-mate's wife pregnant through this procedure. They were all against the gangs in their own way.

Once they got home, Abood planned to let the villagers know of this good news.

"Dear, please prepare some food to serve the villagers tonight. I will go and buy some nuts and raisins too. I will invite them here after tonight's prayers to announce Juliana's pregnancy."

Later that night, the men from the masjid came to Abood's house. Abood invited them in and made the announcement.

"Assalamu alaikum to everyone. I'm glad you all came here tonight. I want to share this good news for us to celebrate. Alhamdulillah, Juliana is now pregnant with Omar's child."

Everyone was happy to hear the news and thanked Allah, and congratulated each other. This baby that Juliana conceived was a symbol of their fight against the gangs. In one aspect, they had won.

The head of the village asked permission to speak and said,

"This success is only a small step towards a bigger one. I hope everyone will continue to be supportive to Omar and his just cause by giving help to Juliana. We will all take care of her all along her pregnancy."

Love flowed in Abood's house that night. Deeply touched, Juliana thanked Abood, the head of the village and also to everyone present. She wished that Omar was with her then.

Meanwhile, Omar was hoping to hear news on Juliana, it would help him bear the hardship of being in the prison. Three visits passed and none came to see him. He kept telling himself to be patient and wait for another week. On the fourth week, Juliana finally went to

the prison. The moment she entered, drawing a big smile, Omar knew that she brought good news. The one he had been waiting to hear. A soon as she sat down on the chair, and Omar asked her quietly "Are you pregnant?" She nodded. "Yes, I'm pregnant now, and we will get the baby after nine months". Omar felt like flying in the air. He told her that he would endure the brutality of the jailers till he got his freedom and nothing would stop him from struggling to restore his ancestors' land. And he would never give up the right to return to their village.

Once the news of Juliana's pregnancy spread in the village, everyone offered Juliana help even for the slightest of task. Young children offered to run errand for her, she needn't even go to the shop to get her basic needs. Womenfolk helped with her chores and some even began knitting some baby clothes, since the baby would arrive somewhere in the winter.

At night when she was all alone, Juliana felt the need to talk to someone. She caressed her abdomen and talked to her baby in the womb.

"Mama don't know whether you're a boy or a girl. If you are a girl, mama will dress you up like a princess and teach you like grandmother used to teach mama. You will learn to cook delicious food, sewing and also beading. Mama will also teach you to make the best cheese in the world. Most important is that you will learn to respect and appreciate others." And then she could feel the baby responding by giving a kick.

At other times, she talked to the baby as though it was a boy.

"You will carry on the flag of Palestine. Be courageous like your baba. Stand up for your rights and always respect your elders. I don't know how to teach you to do boys' stuff with your baba in prison but I am sure there are many who are willing to help you become the best in your field."

The days had passed swiftly for Juliana, but they dragged like a tortoise walking to Omar. He was suffering from the barbarity of the jailers and their bad treatment. They used all different types of torture to stop him demanding his rights as a human in the prison. Juliana kept rising his morals and strengthening his steadfastness. She told him that the freedom was coming closer by every visit.

Months flew by, Juliana had most of the baby things ready with the help of so many people. She had been experiencing the early signs of approaching labour. She can feel that she waddled more with every movement. She could almost imagine herself making the duckling dance even to go to the bathroom. She smiled at the thought.

One cold morning, that winter, Juliana felt a constricting pain on her lower abdomen. The pains came in a consistent interval, Juliana felt the signs of delivery; so, she went to Rina and told her that her time to deliver was very near. The latter told her husband and they decided to take her to the nearest clinic in the village. That evening, Juliana gave birth to a beautiful baby. Her hair was unlike her mother's. She had curly dark hair but her skin was so fair. Her eyes too followed her father's, very clear light brown eyes. Her fingers and toes were all perfect and her cries were the sweetest thing to Juliana's ears. How Juliana wished that Omar was with her when she delivered but she knew it was just a wishful thinking. She was glad she was with the people who loved her.

They were all happy about the new girl who will be proud of her father who fights against the oppressors and spent years of his age in the prison for the sake of his homeland. Abood asked Juliana about the name she would give her baby. She told him that she will not name her till she visited Omar and he would choose a name for their baby.

Celebrations for the arrival of the new baby girl united the villagers once again. Abood slaughtered a lamb for her sake as ask of by the Islamic religion. Food was prepared by the women. They all contributed in buying the raw materials and groceries for the feast. The baby was well covered in clothes knitted to resemble the Palestinian flag. She looked so lovely.

Some of the younger girls thought she was a doll and wanted to touch her pinkish cheeks. One of them even tried to carry her before an elderly lady stopped her before she could do so.

After two weeks, they all went to visit Omar and brought along the baby to show him. Tears of happiness flowed down Omar's cheeks to see his child. They all started crying because Omar wasn't able to hug his child and the jailer banned him from kissing his baby. He passed his fingers from the small window to touch the child's hair and face. Juliana's heart sank when she saw this but she had to put up a strong face.

Abood reminded Omar about naming his child. He told him that he had asked Juliana to name her but she refused and instead wanted him to give her a name.

"Why don't you name her, Juliana?" Omar asked Juliana.

"I give you the honour of giving her the name, dear".

"As you wish, my love," Omar kept silent for some moments then he said that he adores his homeland Palestine therefore he decided to name her Falastin which means Palestine.

6 MARRIAGE

When the invasion happened Omar and Juliana were in high school. Circumstances made them leave school and they were suddenly forced to become adult. Reflecting his life in imprisonment, Omar decided he should make education, his main weapon in fighting the oppressors.

It was the seventh year of the prison sentence. Omar decided to complete his study inside the prison. He told Juliana to register him at a school and asked her to bring him the books to study. She was glad that he would complete his studies and she encouraged him to make such a step. Juliana was looking after the baby and at the same time she was working in the field to save more money. She spent only on the basic necessities and save the rest for Omar's study needs.

Omar was thinking about the ways to defeat the gangs and to make people aware of their occupation which stole the Palestinian lands and kill the innocent Palestinians. On top of that, he wanted to prove that Palestine was very much populated land and not as the gangs claimed it to be that is a land without people and all ready for them to live in.

The situation continued to get harder for Omar. The gangs had just decided to ban all visitors to the prison. They did all the thing possible to annoy the Palestinian prisoners. They listened to no one. They had no empathy for anyone. Juliana tried several times to visit Omar but to no avail. As for Omar, to not be able to see his wife was already hard enough to bear. But to not able to see Falastin, the apple of his eyes as well, had been too much for him to suffer. To make it worse the treatment he received from the jailers became more torturous each day.

Juliana on the other hand, was spending nights crying and worrying about her husband. She kept thinking of how she could help him while at the same time, nurturing Falastin with all the values she had dreamt of when the baby was still inside her womb. Falastin grew up pretty much like an orphan without her father by her side.

While singing lullabies for her baby, Juliana's tears trickled down her cheeks. The memories with her parents rushed back. She remembered when she was five years old, she had sat on her father's shoulders in the field.

"Look around, Juliana," he said as he moved in circles. "All these will be yours when I die. Take good care of them just as I've done, and as my father and his father before him had done. This field will provide us food, clothes, education and the rest of our needs."

All of that had gone, Baba. I had lost everything, even you and Mama. Juliana wiped away her tears.

She remembered looking intently at her mother and listened well when she cooked. Her beautiful mother spoke softly, teaching her what to do next, how to make falafil, kefta, musakhan and other delicious Palestinian food including making the dips like hummus and ghanoush. Her mother taught her how to behave like a lady and instilled in her strong-minded qualities.

Coming back to reality, she stroked Falastin's wavy dark hair. She told herself to be strong and she had to be both mother and father to the innocent girl, while her father was still in the prison. Sometimes a pang of jealousy rushed through her when she saw young couples about her age with their children in the park or at the stores. Quickly, she brushed it off. She kept saying to herself, "Falastin has a father whom she can be proud of; a fighter for their homeland."

After years in prison, Omar had grown from a spirited teenager to a wiser man, but still just as spirited. Never for once did he regret his decision to join Sami and the other demonstrators on the day he was caught by the gangs. He had been through so much; he even fathered a beautiful girl whom he had never kissed, hugged nor carried. In spite of all the hardships, Omar managed to get his High School Certificate after two years. He was contented with his achievement because he had utilized the time and achieved success while being imprisoned. However, anger remained inside him because the privilege of seeing his family was taken away. Such matter could easily threw him out of control when he was younger, but being wiser now, he channelled his frustrations and bitterness into learning handcrafts. He was skillful at that. He made a lot of presents for Juliana and his daughter. He would give them these presents when the ban on visitation was lifted.

Omar learnt the Hebrew language through some books and he practiced it by arguing with the jailers to show them that the Palestinians were well-educated too. He told them about the history of Palestine and the ancient nations who lived in it. He proved many times that Palestine was for Palestinians who had been lived there a long time ago. Omar even spent his time reading books about the Jewish history to be able to debate with them and bring evidences from their own books.

Although his prison terms almost came to an end, Omar still couldn't get used to not having visitation rights. Weeks change to months and months to year, Omar was still hoping to see his family. However, he saw no end to that situation. He could endure all physical torture but not being able to see his wife and child was just too much for him. After a lot of thinking, he decided to stage a hunger strike to demand his rights. He intended to make the jailers obliged and put an end to the unfair treatment he received. The jailer presented him food from under the cell door but Omar refused to take it. The jailer was surprised and asked Omar,

"Why don't you want to eat?"

Then Omar replied

"I will start a hunger strike and I will not eat anything except water and salt till you let my family visit me."

The tough jailer opened the cell and started beating Omar, forcing him to eat. When Omar still didn't give in, the jailer finally brought him water and salt.

"As you wish, here, take the salt and water! We'll see how long you can last on these. We'll see how tough you are. Then, when you ask for food, let me laugh the loudest at you!"

During the first week, Omar lost a few kilograms off his weight. He started suffering from pain and illness. He became very weak after two weeks. The jailer brought him delicious food to make him eat but all the attempts was futile.

"Here, take this favourite food of yours. I know your kind like to eat this delicious lamb maqluba so much. You have been dying to eat this since you came to stay here, right? Don't deny it. Have a bite," said the jailer not giving up.

Omar didn't even look at the mentioned food. After a month, he became very thin and his eyes sank deep in his face. He only felt lazy and tired. He wasn't able to stand on his feet and he became like a zombie, the living dead.

Looking at him like that, the gangs moved him to their hospital to be treated. They were planning to force feed him through his nostrils. He still refused to cooperate with the doctors. Finally, after six month of hunger strike, Omar succeeded in his attempt. His family would be allowed to visit him provided he ends his hunger strike. A month later, the lawyer surprised Juliana by telling her that she could visit her husband the following Monday. Juliana couldn't contain her delight since she hadn't visited him for two years. Juliana eagerly told Abood and her four years old daughter the great news. Falastin was so excited over the idea of meeting her father at last.

They day they reached the prison, the jailer inspected all of them. Not even a child was spared. With weapons in their hands, little Falastin was terrified. She held on to her mother's hand and gripped hard till they were finally ordered to pass through.

Juliana's tears automatically trailed down her cheeks when she saw Omar's condition after their long separation. He was so thin, just bones and skin. She could even carry him should he fell down. His eyes, however, lit up the moment they settled on his daughter. Falastin was apprehensive at first.

"Mama, where is Baba?" she asked nervously. Her eyes were still searching behind the prison bars.

"I am your Baba, dear. Come closer, please," Omar tried to convince her.

"Yes, Falastin. He is your Baba." Juliana pulled her child to get closer to the bars.

"But Mama... Baba looks different in the picture at home," Falastin said innocently.

Juliana stroked her daughter's beautiful hair gently. "Yes, my darling, Baba wasn't this thin before. He's been very sick."

Finally, Falastin touched her father's bony fingers and pulled to her mouth to kiss it as a sign of respect and love.

It was a very sad and touching moment to watch Omar trying to hug his daughter who was born four years ago. They all started crying and Omar was kissing his daughter with difficulty. He kept saying that he was her father and soon they would meet each other out of this prison. The jailer then came to inform that visiting time was over and instructed them to leave at once. Falastin, who had just got used to seeing her father after so long, cried when she realised they had to leave without him.

"We'll meet again soon!" Omar tried to soothe her.

As they moved out of the meeting room, Falastin turned back and shouted to her father,

"I Goodbye, Baba."

Omar couldn't wait for his prison term to end. He was counting the days when he would be able to live with his wife and daughter peacefully. He tried to spend his time reading newspapers and books. Meanwhile, Juliana was still working in the field to earn money for their family's needs, and especially for Omar to gain his strength back. However, every Monday she took a rest from the job so that she and Falastin could visit Omar. Every time they visited him, Omar gave

Falastin a present he made himself. She loved them all because her father made them especially for her. By then, she had become very close with her father as though they had never separated before.

One day, the lawyer came to Juliana and unexpectedly informed that Omar would finally get his freedom the following Friday. They all had to wait for him outside the prison to take him home. Juliana couldn't believe her ears. She immediately told Falastin and Abood about Omar's release, and finally his freedom. Overjoyed with happiness, Juliana started preparing and tiding their home for Omar's homecoming.

It was Thursday, Juliana and Abood put the Palestinian flags over their homes and decorated the place. They agreed to wake up early the next day for the important trip. In the morning, they drove the car towards the prison and waited outside. They had waited for seven hours, before Omar finally appeared from the prison gate. Juliana ran towards him and hugged him closely, crying with happiness. Abood couldn't stop his tears from flowing when he saw Falastin running and yelling at her father,

"My Baba. My Baba."

Omar cried all the way in the car. "I'm finally going home, Juliana," he managed to say between tears. "It's so nice to breathe the air of pure freedom. I miss this air, this view, this feeling of being a free man."

"Yes dear." Juliana gripped his hand. "Your patience had paid off. You are a free man right from the start. No prison can stop you from fighting for justice. Thank God for everything."

All the while Falastin sat on her father's lap, humming the song her mother sang for her every night before she went to sleep. Sometimes her loose hairs touched her father's cheek and he gently smoothed them down again. For more than four years he had dreamt of holding his child, carrying her, calming her down if she cried, and a lot of other things a father should do. And now she wanted to sit on his lap. He felt such blessings for her to want to do that. Time and again he hugged her closer to his chest.

Omar then said to Abood,

"Uncle Abood, I don't know how to thank you enough for everything that you have done for Juliana and Falastin. And not forgetting for myself since I was caught."

Abood shushed him,

"Don't worry about that Omar, since you started working for me and proved yourself worthy, it is my duty to be beside you because you are like my son. Besides that, now I have someone calling me grandfather," he smiled and lightly patted Falastin's head.

When they reached their home, the villagers came to congratulate and celebrate Omar's freedom. They asked many questions. Sometimes, two or three questions at once. Omar felt like a celebrity, being interviewed by reporters.

"Okay, take a number at the counter and I will answer your questions when your turn comes," he teased and laughter filled the small house.

Omar related how he was tortured in the prison especially when he demanded the rights of Palestinians to live in their ancestors' land and cultivate their own orchards. Having lost his, he was quite vocal about this. Once, his back was almost broken when they hit him with a wooden chair. It was the chair which broke into pieces.

At other times, he was tortured mentally and emotionally. The gangs wanted him to surrender, but he persevered. He told them that they shouldn't give up till the Palestinians restore their stolen land from the gangs. Omar was ready to sacrifice his life for Palestine.

After about a week of his return, Omar was asked by Abood to celebrate his long-postponed marriage party.

"Omar, do you remember when you first came to work with me; you wanted to save money to celebrate your marriage and do a party for the villagers?"

"Of course, Uncle. I have never forgotten about it all this while."

"Shall we make the party next Friday?"

Scratching his not itchy head, Omar answered,

"Oh, no! That's too soon. Juliana and Falastin would need new clothes and I don't think they can make it so fast."

"OK then, you set the date and I'll start the ball rolling. Don't you worry, you will have plenty of help from everyone in the village. They would be glad to do so."

"OK I will discuss this matter with Juliana and we will let you know as soon as possible."

Juliana gave Omar a date a fortnight later for her to get everything ready for the party. Once they set the date, preparations were in progress. They were both anxiously waiting for the wedding day. It would officially make them a new Palestinian family living in the same house.

Abood and his wife reminded Omar and Juliana that the day was drawing nearer. They had to be ready for the party. Friends came to help Omar take care of all that needed to be done, and Juliana with preparing for her new clothes. The ladies also helped her to memorise old Palestinian songs for the party. They wanted her to have a very memorable day and hoped that it would wash away all the sufferings she had endured so far.

Omar wanted his beloved daughter to look outstanding during the party. He asked Juliana whether she can make something for her.

"Juliana, can you sew a new white dress which is decorated with the colours of the Palestinian flag for our daughter?"

Juliana smiled. "I will certainly do that dear. I'll make her a dress like mine. She's going to be my little bridesmaid."

That delighted Omar.

"Thank you very much my darling. I want to make her very happy and proud of her parents' wedding. I would like to compensate her for the years she spent without me."

"I'll do my best, and I want you to carry and dance with her most of the time."

The day before the wedding, Juliana asked all her friends in the refugee home and a few of her friends in the village to come to celebrate a special small party for the bride. Rina too, invited her neighbours to attend Juliana's party. While they gathered at Abood's house,

Juliana asked, "Is there anyone here who can do my hair?"

Samah who sat in the middle, raised her hand. "Yes, I can do all the bride's stuff and I'll make you look and feel like a queen."

Beaming with delight, Juliana asked Samah to come forward to her and hugged the petite lady.

"It will be my dream day tomorrow, so I want to be as bright as a star."

"Certainly." Samah nodded. "I'll do my best to make you look so exquisite."

"Oh, that's great. Please stay back a while after the party so we can discuss further."

"Don't worry. I'll stay with you tonight and we'll start our preparation early tomorrow morning."

At the end of the day, everyone came to Abood's house and Juliana wore her new red dress for the small party before the wedding day and Samah put some makeup on Juliana's face. The young girls started dancing and the old ones began singing the old Palestinian songs while they were clapping. Juliana danced with all the girls who considered her like a sister and family. They were all joyful and glad to participate in Juliana's party.

Falastin was the happiest person there. She had never seen this side of her mother before. She was glad that her father was out of the prison and they can be like a normal family.

On the other hand, Omar invited his friends from the refugee home and Abood asked a few of his friends and close neighbours to join and participate in Omar's party that same night at Omar's house. Abood brought the chairs, strawberry juice and coffee out. Salem, the new caretaker at the refugee home, asked the youths from the home to help, so they cleared the field and arranged the chairs in rows. Some of them prepared the juice while the others set fire to make the coffee. After sunset, the guests started coming to the field. Omar and the youths began singing the old Palestinian songs and danced the dabka. The old men clapped and joined in with the the songs. They spent the whole night singing and dancing. Omar approached Salem and Abood and pulled them over to join the dabka dance.

After some time, Abood went back to his house and asked Juliana, "Is the dinner ready?"

"Almost, in a few more minutes everything will be done," she said.

"OK, I'll bring some of the youths to help serve the food."

Abood told Salem and the boys to bring the dinner over to Omar's house. Their dinner consists of maftoul with chicken and tomato broth. Some boys carried the carbonated drinks in cans to be distributed to the guests.

After their dinner, these guests returned home to come back again the following day for the general lunch. Omar, happy but exhausted from all the dancing, went back to his home to sleep but Juliana and Falastin stayed back at Abood's house.

In the morning, Abood woke Omar up as he needed help to slaughter two lambs. Omar brought along the youths to help Abood cook the rice and meat to serve to the people during the general lunch. The rice was cooked with saffron and other spices, giving out a wonderful aroma. The lambs were seasoned with aromatic herbs, lightly spiced, cooked in yogurt, and baked in an oven. They will then be served with huge quantities of rice. Everyone in the village was invited for the lunch.

On the other hand, Juliana and Samah got up and they started preparing the breakfast and after that Samah cut Juliana's hair to appear in a unique style.

By noon and the guests started arriving for the wedding lunch. Omar and his friends began serving meals to people in the field and the women had theirs at Abood's house. They congratulated Omar and wished him a long and happy life. Lunch over, Omar showered and put on his new black suit while his friends waited outside to start the celebration. The moment Omar came out, they rushed over, singing. One of them carried him on his shoulders. Together with Abood and Salem, they walked in the streets of the village. People threw sweets on them and congratulated Omar. After the walk, they returned to the field and waited till the women finished their party with Juliana.

Inside Abood's house, Juliana wore a very lavish white dress and she put a light makeup on her face. With her new haircut, she looked every bit the ravishing bride she should be. The women gazed at her in awe while she was dancing like a butterfly on flowers. Her friends joined the dance and sang the songs about Palestine. The elders were relieved and thankful that Juliana could finally enjoy her wedding party after all the hardships she had gone through. The party lasted for three hours before Omar came and took Juliana back to their home.

After a week of rest, Omar told Juliana that he would return to work on the field and he will plant more olive trees. He needed to show to the gangs that Palestine belonged to his ancestors. Juliana agreed and offered to help. After all, she was so used to working in the fields during his absence. In the morning, he got up early and went to the field. He started working and Abood was surprised that Omar started working in the field so early.

"Good morning Omar. You are here early?"

"Good morning Uncle. Yes, I plan to start work like before."

"That's good," Abood paused for a moment. "But don't you think that you should continue studies? You should get a university degree and move on to greater heights."

"I intend to do that, Uncle. But I have to work to provide for my family first. Anyway, the fees will be high, I suppose."

"You don't have to worry about the fees, Omar. I will finance your studies until you graduate."

Omar was touched by Abood's words. "Oh, thank you so much, Uncle. But I can't accept that. You've done so much for me and my family whilst I was in prison. I can't afford to burden you with more."

"I insist." Abood stressed. "Please don't worry about your family too. Juliana has always wanted you to get into university. I'm sure she'll agree with me".

Omar couldn't argue more with the man he had much respect and loved as his own father.

He decided to study history to spread the knowledge and life of the Palestinians to all. He registered at a university and studied hard besides working in the fields. Omar didn't waste any time; he brought along books to be read in between chores in the field. Having to compete with students much younger than him, Omar tried his best to get high marks in his exams. Most of his classmates were in awe at his spirit. They became inspired to be better persons after knowing his struggle all these years.

After four years, he graduated with a bachelor degree in history and decided to complete his post-graduate degree later on. Omar worked hard to achieve his goals and to prove that Palestinians are not illiterate and uncivilized people as the gangs claimed. Not long after that, Omar secured a job as an assistant lecturer at one of the Palestinian universities, making their lives more comfortable after that.

By then, Juliana and Omar also had four more children, all boys. Omar was glad that he has more heirs to be raised as patriots in his home country. All the five children, not only studied at schools but also help them in the field as well. Juliana fed them with the spirit of patriotism to be national heroes like their father. Omar encouraged and taught his children the history of Palestine to make them aware of what happened to their country and for them to be keen to defend it when they got older. Looking back at all the hardships he had endured, Omar was thankful he finally had a happy family. The children are obedient and courteous. Almost every day, after prayers, they began their day near the olive trees, enjoying the sounds of the birds chirping freely on the branches above. They usually had olive oil, homemade white cheese and some fresh bread; after grinding the wheat by the old mill, for breakfast.

Omar and Juliana were glad to see their children growing up healthy and strong enough to cultivate the land and do various chores on the field. Omar decided to expand their home because it was too small for all of them. He remembered how the original house was built using his own hands and with Abood's help. Now that he has his own sons, they all helped to make a bigger house for all of them to live comfortably. Their new house was very beautiful. They added a couple more rooms. In addition, Juliana and Falastin planted colourful flowers in the courtyard. Their house really looked wonderful with nice beautiful garden and the olive trees surrounding it. They were all safe from the oppressing gangs who occupied the nearby villages in Palestine.

7 TRAVELLING ABROAD

The news about Palestine was published through radios, televisions, internet and newspapers. People throughout the world hear about the gangs attacking Palestine and Palestinians. They heard about the killings of innocent families, making the Palestinians leave their lands and villages, destroying homes and cutting down trees. As a result, many activists around the world condemn the savage and brutal crimes committed by the gangs. They made small demonstrations worldwide condemning the action of the oppressors and showing solidarity towards this poor nation under attack. They want justice to be held.

The activists began arranging small groups and travel to Palestine in order to defend the Palestinians and face the gangs to stop their crimes.

One day, a group of western activists came to Omar's place and they started meeting people. They made banners against the gangs and they began planning to make demonstrations near the settlements. Omar participated in such events and joined the demonstrations. He met the activists and explained to them about Palestine and the stolen lands and the gangs' crimes. A few days after knowing this group of activists, Omar invited them to have dinner at his home.

"I was with this group of enthusiastic activists this morning," he told Juliana as soon as he reached home. "They seemed like a nice group of people earnestly wanting to help for our cause. So, I really hope you don't mind that I have invited them for dinner."

His wife's eyes widened. "Oh, really? What could we serve them with such a short notice?" "Well, whatever we're having for dinner. Just make extra for about five people. Don't bother to make anything special. They're coming mostly to hear my experience being in the prison. You don't have to cook anything fancy, my dear."

Juliana smiled with a relief. "OK then. I hope they don't mind eating our humble food."

Just after sunset and Omar finished his daily obligatory prayers, the activists arrived. Omar welcomed them and invited them to sit outside the house, a lightly lit place under a big, old olive tree. They asked Omar about his family and the history of Palestine.

Omar talked about the country called Palestine where people of different faith had been living harmoniously for ages. All that changed when the hooligans were brought in from the big land. Then people started losing lands and lives. Omar continued to tell of the gangs' crimes, the tragic experience of losing his family and the hardship of his early life. History being his core subject, he told them all these with ease.

"Do you know that I was sent to prison at the age of 17, just for joining a demonstration?" Omar questioned his guests.

"Oh, my God! Really?" William, one of the guests, replied with a shock in his voice. "You were so young then!"

Omar nodded. "In that incident, we lost Uncle Sami, the man whom we loved so dearly. He invited us, the orphans, to live in his house and he took care of us like his own children although he himself had never been married. He was shot only once, but that day we lost him forever. I, too, was shot in the leg and fell down. They dragged me into their custody before any of my friends could help me."

The activists inhale sharply, aghast over hearing first-hand experience from an ex-prisoner. It was different from the news propagated by the western media which accused the Palestinians for initiating the harsh treatment towards the settlers. They were told that the world should sympathize with the gang for having been disturbed with the demonstrations. In actual fact, they were the ones disturbing the peaceful lives of the Palestinians in the first place.

Omar also related stories from his prison days and the bad and inhumane treatment received by the Palestinian prisoners.

After a few moments of silence, William spoke,

"Would you mind if we invite you to come and study in England?"

Omar's face lit up. "I don't mind at all. It's my dream to complete my post degree and work as a professor at any one of the Palestinian universities."

William looked right at him, "When we return to England, we will register you at one of the British universities, what would you like to study Mr. Omar?"

"I would like to study Palestinian history further because I want to write books about Palestine and spread the truth." Omar explained.

"Good. We will do our best to help you", William said.

Omar then asked Juliana to bring the food and he started telling the activists about the Palestinian dishes and how they were cooked. After dinner, the guests took their leave and promised they would stay in contact. They were all please about the meeting and the hospitality of the poor Palestinians.

The next morning, Omar was working in the farm and Abood came to help him irrigate the trees. Omar related to him about the activists' visit and also informed him about their offer to help him study abroad. Abood was clearly happy to hear such news.

"I will also support you. I'll send you money and take care of your family," he said enthusiastically.

Omar was relieved to hear such assurance. "Again, I thank you so much for your offer. Let's wait and see what the coming days will bring. However, I do hope that I could get some kind of financial aid from the university to help ease the burden," Omar replied.

The aroma of the bread Juliana baked really made them hungry, they soon asked for breakfast. While eating, Abood asked Omar to take care of the farm because he would visit his relatives in the nearby village for a week.

When Abood came back a week later, he received a call from England. William wishing to talk to Omar. Abood asked him to call again after 10 minutes. He should get Omar to answer the phone himself. When William called the second time, Omar was already at Abood's house. William told him to send all his related papers in order to register him at the university. Filled with excitement, Omar sprinted home to deliver the news. Juliana gave her assurance and support and would do her best to work and take care of the children.

Omar prepared his papers and went to the post office. He told the employee that he needed to send his papers to his friend in England via the fastest mode. The employee suggested he do express mail but for a higher fee. Needing to send them fast, he paid for the express mail. The employee also wished all the best to him.

Two weeks later, William again contacted Omar and told him the news that he was accepted at the university. William also promised that he will assist with the visa application. Omar expressed his greatest appreciation for William's help. He told Juliana that he would be traveling to England soon. He prepared his bag and waited for the visa.

A month later, the postman knocked at the door and Omar came out to him. The postman asked, "Are you Omar?"

Omar said "Yes, it's me. How can I help you?"

The postman handed him a parcel. "This just arrived from England and addressed to you." Omar grinned instantly. "Oh, thank you so much! I have been waiting for this." He quickly opened the parcel and rushed inside to inform Juliana about the visa he just received. Next, he rushed to Abood. They were all very happy about that.

During dinner that night, Omar broke the news to his children.

"Children, I shall be leaving for England soon. My application for a student visa to that country as a student had been approved and is now with me. My bags are all packed and ready to go as soon as Rafah Port opens."

He noted the instant tears in Falastin's eyes.

"My dear Falastin, please don't be sad." He quickly said. "I know you are a big and strong girl now. I would only be gone for a little while. It won't be as long as the prison term I served before. I am going to study History so that I can write the truth about our country. Don't you worry, I'm going there as a free man. You can help mama to take care of your younger siblings, can't you? I, Omar, hereby raised you to be second-in-command of this great family."

Last of her tears trickled down her cheeks and her earlier gloomy face lit up. A smile appeared, enhanced by sweet dimples.

"Alright, baba. Please promise to come home as soon as you finish your studies. I miss you already."

All her younger siblings got up and hugged their father. One after another, Omar kissed them on their cheeks. Although he didn't show, Omar already felt like crying. How would he survive in a foreign country without his wife who was his strength and life, and also his children, his life's treasures? May Allah guide him always and may his endeavours be easy.

Omar kept listening to the news to know when Rafah port on the Egyptian side would be opened to let the passengers leave Palestine. After a week, the much-awaited news was spread. Rafah crossing would be opened only for the students and patients on Wednesday for three days. On Tuesday, Omar made a final check on his documents and bags. He had to leave his village at dawn to reach Rafah Crossing in the morning. As they put the luggage in the car, Abood reminded Omar to focus on his studies and spread the truth about Palestine. Juliana hugged Omar. Despite the welling in her eyes, she gave him all the encouragement he needed.

"You are not going into a prison, Omar. So, don't worry about me and the children. Uncle Abood is always there if I need any help. You just concentrate on your studies and come back with better knowledge."

Omar hugged her back. "I know, my dear. This isn't going to be a parting, but merely a temporary absence on my part in your life and the lives of our children."

One by one his children kissed his hands and hugged him. They understood that their father was going abroad for a meaningful purpose. They promised to do their needful chores and help their mother always. After everyone bid their farewell, Omar got into the car and told the driver to drive-off.

Omar reached Rafah port when the sun was already shining brightly. He entered the passengers' hall to get his papers done. That made him wait from seven in the morning till five in the evening. Rafah crossing was full of students and patients. Omar met a patient who wanted to leave for Cairo for a surgical operation on her legs. She was an old lady travelling all by herself. Omar first noticed her crying as he was moving in the queue. He went over to her and asked her why she was crying. She said the pain in her legs were unbearable and she had difficulties moving along in the queue. So, Omar offered to help her get the papers ready for clearance to leave for Cairo. Once both, his and the old lady's papers were approved, he offered her to travel in the same car with him.

Feeling grateful, the old lady thanked Omar.

"I really appreciate what you have done, my son. Without your help, I might have to wait until tomorrow. I have no one with me to help."

"Don't mention it. It is my duty as a fellow citizen of Palestine to help one another in the hour of need. Here, let me help carry your bags."

Omar helped the lady got out of the hall and he stopped an Egyptian car to take them to Cairo. He told the driver to send the old lady to the hospital and then continue their journey to the airport. During the long journey to Cairo, which took more than six hours, they talked about life circumstances in Palestine and their experience about wars. Omar related all his tragic childhood experience and the harsh treatments from the gang he had endured. The old lady was sympathetic towards him.

Finally, they reached the hospital and Omar helped the old lady by bringing a wheelchair from the hospital gate and asked the driver to help him put the lady on it. Then he took the lady and her luggage inside the hospital and asked the nurses to take care of her, as she was on her own. Satisfied that she was in good hands, Omar then continued his journey to the airport.

Upon arrival, collected his luggage from the car and proceeded to the counter at the departure hall. It was already 2 am. Although tired because it was almost 24 hours since he left home, he felt enthusiastic about his journey. He showed his passport and ticket to the Egyptian officer who then let Omar pass into the departure hall. As Omar entered, he found some Palestinian passengers sitting together and he sat down beside them.

All three of them were waiting for their flight to Ukraine. They are going to register as medical students at Vinnitsa National Pirogov

Memorial Medical University.

They must have scored very high marks in their Tawjeehee exams. Brilliant students, they are. Omar felt proud seeing younger generation of Palestinians able to venture into such field of study. He talked to them and congratulated them for getting a place in that university. When they left him to board their plane, Omar waited patiently for his.

At six o'clock in the morning, his turn came. He is quite nervous but excited at the same time. In the name of Allah, the most merciful the most compassionate, Omar prayed as he set his right foot first on the plane. Being on his first journey out of his country and first experience on an airplane, he had to be thankful to the Almighty Allah. He had suffered so much before and now, as a free man he is able to travel anywhere. In his long journey on the airplane; more than five hours, Omar reflected upon his life journey. Once in a while he dozed off due to sleepiness and exhaustion. In one of those moments, he dreamt of the rock where he used to sit with Julianna when they brought their sheep to feed on the green grass of home. He could visualize everything clearly when he woke up. Oh, how peaceful life was at that time! And how innocent they both were. Now Juliana is his wife and they have their own children. How thankful he was for all that.

When the pilot announced that they will be landing in half an hour, Omar went to the toilet to freshen up. He wouldn't want his friend, William to see his unkempt look.

William and his friends were waiting at the airport to welcome Omar; they were carrying the Palestinian flags. As soon as Omar arrived and walked out of the gate, they rushed over and hugged him, they carried him on their shoulders. Omar wasn't expecting such warm welcome for him. Being on their shoulder made him feel like a real hero.

William welcomed him to his house. He introduced Omar to his parents. They were delighted to see him in person as their son had been talking about 'Omar' since his return from Palestine.

"Welcome to our humble home, Omar. I hope you will be satisfied with our hospitality," said William's father as he shook hands with Omar.

"Thank you, sir. I can't be more honoured," Omar responded. "I appreciate everything that William has done for me. Making my dream of pursuing post graduate studies abroad a reality and now extending his home for my stay. Thank you so much again to all of you. May you be rewarded abundantly."

William invited everyone to the table for some meal he had bought earlier and reheated by his mother.

"Don't worry, brother," William said. "I bought these from a Muslim shop downtown. Since coming back from Palestine, I've learned about Muslim halal food and I even eat them myself."

"I can never thank you enough, brother. Your hospitality is superb. May Allah bless you always."

After their meal, Omar excused himself to get some rest and sleep. The guest room William prepared for Omar was cosy, and as soon as Omar's head hit the pillow he fell asleep. He hadn't sleep properly for over two days.

In the evening, they went for a walk around London city and had dinner at one of the old restaurant in the downtown. They planned to go to the university in the morning.

At eight in the morning the next day, William came to Omar's room.

"Good morning, Omar," he greeted. "Did you sleep well?"

Omar smiled his, way, "Good morning my dear friend. Yes, I slept soundly throughout the night."

William laughed.

"We have just prepared breakfast. Hopefully you could prepare for us some Palestinian food tomorrow. I miss the delicious food we tasted there."

"Of course. I am ever willing to teach you how to cook some of the dishes soon."

"Great! Let's get our breakfast, and be on our way."

After breakfast, Omar changed his clothes and wore the Palestinian kuffeya around his neck, a symbol of his nation. They reached London University and William introduced Omar to his friends there. They all welcomed Omar and they showed him respect and solidarity. Omar was so happy to meet such people who appreciated the Palestinians.

William took Omar to confirm his registration. He next took Omar to be introduced to the professors. Most of the professors welcomed Omar and offered their help when needed. At the office of the Dean of the Faculty of History, Omar and William were told to have their seats. The professor then gazed at Omar and asked,

"Is all the news we heard from William about Palestine true?

"Yes, it is. Omar answered. "But we heard that the western media show the opposite side and manipulates the truth."

The professor nodded. "William told me that you lived in one of the Palestinian villages and had witnessed and experienced the conflict and crimes against your people."

Omar replied calmly, "Yes, I lost all my family there. The gangs killed and destroyed everything..." He briefly related what actually happened to the Palestinians.

"We left everything behind us with hope that we would be able return to our village. But as of this moment, all that remains a dream."

Leaning over his desk, the professor said "Mr. Omar, I am planning to make a research about the Palestinian-Israeli conflict and show the truth to the western people. I hope that you'll help me in my research."

Lifting both his hands, Omar said "With open arms, sir. I would really like to do that because I came here to study history and write books and show the world how miserable life has been in Palestine after the Israeli occupation on our lands. How they violate human rights carelessly."

The professor thanked Omar and William. He said to Omar,

"My office is open for you anytime and we'll start the research soon. Thanks to you too, William."

The university session started and Omar began attending the lectures. He tried to attend all of them without skipping any. He remained polite with his professors and worked hard in his studies. Omar turned out to be the distinguished few amongst his colleagues especially after he had got high marks during the quizzes and tests. He began writing researches about Palestinian history and the professors highly admired him for his works.

Omar kept in touch with his family in Palestine through Abood's home phone. They kept on encouraging and supporting him. In addition to that, William and his family were always there beside Omar to offer him a comfortable atmosphere to study well. They encouraged him to excel by giving everything he needed for his research. They reminded him all the time that his family were waiting for him to come back and make them proud.

During Omar's study at London University, he made a lot of western friends from different countries in Europe. They loved Omar as their brother and they invited him to their homes. Omar obliged and used these opportunities to brief them about Palestine and the sufferings of its people. He tried to make them see the truth through his live experiences. They all showed sympathy and solidarity to Omar and Palestine. They would plan convoys with food and other goods to visit and help Palestinians.

One day, one of the hosts, a Spanish man, sympathetically said,

"It is very unfortunate for you to have undergone such torturous and barbaric treatment when you were still a teenager. I really pity you to have lost your loved ones in those growing up years. I wish time could be reversed and that you didn't have to bear all those pain, Omar".

"It's OK, my brother. We could not reverse time," Omar responded. "I have endured such pain and that made me a stronger person. Also, in the prison I had gained my high school certificate, learned to speak Hebrew and also did many craft work. By the way, I also had a daughter whilst I was in prison."

He went on to share how he and Juliana bravely made it possible. The host and his friends were in awe at her ingenuity. They were all praising her. That made Omar prouder of his loving wife.

At times Omar made small gatherings with his friends inside the university garden. He clarified the history of Palestine and showed them photos of his village and other Palestinian villages. He explained the humanity, hospitality, and steadfastness of the Palestinians.

Once, while Omar was talking to his friends about Palestine, a Zionist sat down near them and he started to argue and interrupt Omar's speech by telling people around Omar that Palestine was their land, by right and they didn't kill any Palestinian there. Omar quickly responded declaring that Palestine belongs to the people of Palestine and the Zionists came and stole the lands by killing the innocents, cutting the trees and destroying their homes and villages.

"You killed all my father, mother, brothers and sisters in front of my eyes. You killed my Christian neighbours and you can see the photos about the crimes you committed."

They began shouting at each other and the university security guard came and asked them to leave. Omar never felt such anger, since his imprisonment days. His friends had to cool him down. They brought him to the rural areas to enjoy the serenity of living in such area without the hustle bustle of city. That ambience brought his memory to his current hometown.

Day after day, Omar made more friends. They asked him to hold meetings and invited him to give lectures on the history of Palestine because many students have never heard about the country. So, Omar discussed with William about his intention to arrange meetings inside the university and he needed the consent of the university administration. They went together to the Dean of the faculty of History and told him about their plan. The professor encouraged him and told Omar that he would offer all facilities to hold these meetings. Omar planned to hold the first meeting on the following Monday and he invited the professor to attend it. Feeling happy, they went home.

In the evening, Omar asked William to provide him with photos that he took while he was in Palestine. They both prepared the materials which he would illustrate and explain to the audience. He went through everything a couple of times to make sure he got all the facts and photos supporting them and got ready for his first meeting.

He printed the invitations and distributed them to the professors and colleagues. He stuck it on the board of the faculty and outside in the centre of the university. In the morning of that Monday, Omar and his friends went to the university hall and prepared the projector and other necessary stuff.

People began to arrive at the hall well before the meeting started. The hall became full of students and professors. Precisely at the time of the agenda, Omar welcomed the audience and started explaining his objective for holding the meeting. He went on to explain about the early history of Palestine before the Israeli occupation of Palestine. In addition to that, he showed them through the projector some old photos about the Palestinian cities and other photos about the Israeli crimes against the Palestinians. He illustrated the amount of destruction of villages by the hands of the Zionist gangs. The meeting lasted for two hours before Omar held questions and answers session. It was opened for debate. Omar ended the meeting by saying that the truth will prevail and Palestine will be free. William and all Omar's friends thanked Omar for his great efforts to spread the knowledge about Palestine.

After the success of that first meeting, Omar was invited to talk at other universities as well. He did all those with pleasure. He had almost achieved what he intended to do before coming to England, that was to spread the truth about Palestine.

It was the final year at the university and Omar finished his studies and graduated. Since his family couldn't attend his graduation, Omar invited William's family to replace them. They were proud to be invited. Omar thanked them for all the things they had given him, financial aid, and emotional support and just by being there for him at his hour of needs.

William threw a graduation as well as farewell party for Omar that night. Every guest greeted Omar and some of them gave some cash for him. He thanked them all for the opportunity to just be there and study. He then invited them to be his guest and the chance for him to show them the hospitality Palestinians would offer.

Omar couldn't wait to go home to his family. Just a day after graduation, he was already on the plane back to Cairo.

8 DEATH

The breeze blew from the east. The morning sun rose to add its warmth to the weather and covered the green fields. The blue sky indicated pureness and quietness. People were ready and spirited to start a new day. Students were moving to their schools; farmers on their way to the fields. The younger children gathered and played about in the streets.

Omar was on his way home from England. The plane landed safely at Cairo airport. He went past the immigration officer without much hassle and walked out to the arrival hall. Behind him, he heard loud squeals of laughter. Turning his head, he saw the reason for the noise. A group of teenagers were so excited upon seeing their friends or family waving at them on the left corner of the arrival hall.

How lucky of them being waited upon arrival by the loved ones. Oh well, I'll just give a call to surprise Julian. Omar took out his newly acquired mobile phone, a gift from William, and dialled up a number. He knew a telephone had just been installed in their home a few weeks earlier.

"Omar's residence. Juliana here," came the response from the other end.

Oh, how he missed that sweet voice. "Salam, my dearest. Your husband here."

Juliana was so excited to receive a call from her darling husband.

"How are you Omar? Is everything ok over there?" Juliana asked, not knowing that she would unite with her husband in several hours.

"I'm fine. Right now, I'm walking out of the arrival hall in Cairo," he stopped for a while when he heard his wife's shrieks.

"What? You're in Cairo? Are you serious?" Juliana continued after her shrieks.

"Yes, dear. I couldn't waste any time as I heard that the port would be opened today. I will try to get a car to Rafah as soon as possible. The earliest I could arrive is in seven hours from now. Please tell our children and Uncle Abood to wait for me at the Palestinian side of Rafah port"."I'll do so, right away!"

The connection ended before Omar could talk further.

Juliana had immediate plans in her head as women always did. Number one in her checklist

was to let Uncle Abood know of Omar's arrival.

"Assalam, Uncle Abood," she greeted over the phone.

"Wa alaikum Salam, my dear. Is everything fine with you and the children?"

"We're all fine, thank you. How are you?"

"We're fine too. Is everything alright?"

"Yes Uncle, things couldn't be more perfect today. Omar is coming home tonight, he is already in Cairo,"

Abood too was excited, he almost shouted, "Alhamdulillah. All praises be to Allah. I will go and fetch him at Rafah port,"

"Uncle, can you please bring my children along with you? Omar requested that you and the children wait for him at the Palestinian side of Rafah port."

"Alright my dear. Tell them to get ready and I'll be leaving in about five hours' time."

"OK. I will ask them to wear nice clothes. Meanwhile, I'll prepare food and get the house nice and ready."

As soon as he put down the phone, Abood called for his wife. "Rina...Rina! Come here quickly. I have good news!" Abood waved. Rina came rushing to check what the commotion was all about.

"What is it? Come on tell me, what did you mean by good news?" she asked.

"The good news is...Omar is coming home tonight! Isn't it great?"

"Really? Alhamdulillah. Juliana must be very happy then. Can I go over to her house and help her make preparations to welcome him home?"

"Of course, you should, my dear."

Several hours later, Abood put on his suit and his Palestinian Kuffeya around his neck. He waited for Omar's sons and daughter to join him. After seeing them off, Juliana returned home and prepared some Palestinian sweets and made coffee.

Abood drove to Rafah port. They have ample time when they reached it. After waiting several minutes in the car, Abood told the children to stay put while he went to check on Omar at the arrival hall. He searched for Omar everywhere. He walked up the alleyway, he still couldn't find the one face he been waiting for so long to kiss. The one he missed so much, as a son. Again, he paced down the alleyway in search of the figure he longed to hug. Omar was nowhere to be seen. While continuing his search, Omar suddenly appeared from a distance. The moment Omar saw Abood, he ran to the man whom he loved as his father. They hugged each other and tears trickled down their cheeks. Omar kissed Abood's forehead and cheeks, tears and all. When they finally let go of each other, Abood said, "I miss you so much my son. How are you?"

Omar wiped the remaining tears on his cheeks.

"I am fine, thank you, Uncle. I miss all of you and most of all I miss my country."

"Alhamdulillah for your safe arrival." Abood reached for one of Omar's luggage. Coming back from England he bought many things to distribute as souvenirs for his close family and friends.

"Yes," continued Omar, "I am so thankful to the Almighty God for all the good things I have had this past few years. I promise to give back as much as I can to our people and our country."

"It is good that you have such thought."

As they walk towards the car, Abood said," Come quickly, I have a surprise for you".

"What is it?" Omar responded in a curious tone.

Abood signalled towards the car. "Come and see for yourself!"

They almost reached the car when Falastin opened the door of the car and dashed out to hug her father, followed by all her brothers. Seeing their overjoyed reaction, tears of happiness wet Omar's cheeks once again.

"I thought you didn't bring them along!" He said to Abood. "When I saw you alone in the arrival hall, I felt a bit disheartened that you didn't bring any of my children with you, and I didn't think for a moment that they were my surprise."

Falastin and her brothers asked a lot of questions to the father on their journey home.

"Baba, is it true, like mama told us, the people at your university respected you even though you are not a rich person?"

"Yes, my son, when I speak in the lecture hall they kept silenced and paid attention to me. I had the chance to let them know the truth about the current situation in our country. I don't want them to just hear the news from the media, which most of the time are not the truth."

Falastin, further question her father, "How was their respond when they knew how you were treated in the jail?"

"My dear Falastin, I didn't expect they would empathized with me initially, but I even got some of the attendees to shed some tears hearing how I was tortured here. They also praised your mother for her genius idea on how to conceive you." Omar and Juliana had never kept a secret about how they got her and Falastin felt special about it. She was proud of both of her parents.

The long journey felt short because of the time well spent between them. Finally, they reached home where Juliana had been anxiously waiting. She gave her husband a long tearful hug. The way she had the house decorated to welcome him truly impressed and touched Omar. He missed all her nice cooking, so, when he saw the dishes on the table, he ate with gusto. That made Juliana cry thankful tears to be able to prepare her husband's favourites again. That night she and the children gathered around Omar to hear all about his journey to further his education. All five children have set their mind that one day, they too will go to England like their father. They promised Omar that they will be the best in their studies and they will make both, him and their mother proud of their achievements.

A week later, the family was working in the field, it was harvesting time. The trees were full of olives. They worked and had breakfast together before Omar left for his lectures at the university. Juliana urged her children to continue harvesting the fruits so that they could finish before their father returned home. They needed no force nor encouragement to do it because they enjoyed doing it so much.

The Palestinians were about to enjoy the beginning of their day, they heard about the enemy planes dropping bombs on Palestinian camps and the resistance areas. The sound of explosions was heard everywhere, turning it almost like the doomsday where people had no idea where to escape. Several planes attacked at the same time and many martyrs fell down terrifying the young ones and adults alike. Mothers searched for their children in the streets. Injured casualties and martyrs filled the hospitals. Blood was everywhere and the smell of death appeared very close and distinct.

After several hours, the opposition army started land incursion using tanks and they moved towards the Palestinian villages. They had various kinds of weapons and tanks. One of the villagers ran towards Omar's land and shouted at them to safe themselves. He told them that the gangs killed anyone who stood in their way and destroyed the fields. They cut and burn olive trees and bulldozed away the houses.

Juliana quickly took the children home and told them to remain inside. "Don't be afraid of them," she said. At that moment, Omar came back from the university and he was shocked to find his family not in the field. He went home and knocked on the door. Juliana opened it with a worried face. "Have you heard about the gangs?" she asked right away.

"I'm not sure about the news, but the gangs could reach the village soon. Let's not panic anyway. We'll wait for further news."

They stayed home and waited for more news on the radio. The neighbours were truly scared. They all knew what the gang did to their parents and ancestors. Some of the villagers had left the village and escaped to a nearby town to return in the morning. Somehow, they were caught up by the gangs and killed on their way to safety. Omar refused to leave and decided to stay as he knew they would face the same fate. Furthermore, they had small children and couldn't move fast or quiet enough. He would rather die in his home with his family. Juliana tried to maintain her composure and made dinner as usual. The family ate dinner more quietly than usual; eating slowly. Not long after that Juliana ushered her children to sleep.

It was after midnight. The children were sleeping while Omar and Juliana stayed awake to monitor the situation. They started hearing sounds of heavy firing. Falastin awake and screamed all of a sudden, "They will kill us!". Omar and Juliana calmed her down. "You are a Palestinian, so, you must not be afraid of them". The rest of the children woke up as well upon hearing their sister's scream. They too, couldn't sleep, scared of the loud sound of bullets and explosions. Omar and Juliana tried to calm the children down and they all stayed together in one room. The enemy planes were hovering at low levels, they were targeting some fields and homes with their heavy bombs. They sounded louder and nearer. Minutes later, a very big explosion lit up the night outside and shook their house. The children screamed. Too shaken herself, Juliana could no longer calm them.

Omar went to the front door to check what was going on outside. When he opened it, he found their fields all destroyed and burnt. Suddenly, the power was cut and darkness covered the whole village. Juliana began to cry in silent, not wanting the children to hear it. Very much in stress, Omar lit a candle in the room and kept his family ready should anything happen.

Towards dawn, another loud noise came from the field, Omar crept to the door and peeked through the keyhole. He was shocked to see the gangs razing and cutting the olive trees. He started to cry because he had raised the trees like his own children. He quickly returned to Juliana and told her about what he had seen.

"Don't worry, if we stayed alive, we'll plant the field again". She said in her calmest voice. Omar went to check again, this time he saw the trees in flames. By that time, the gangs had captured some of the villagers who still remained in their homes. Omar watched in horror as the gangs killed and tortured the innocent villagers.

Suddenly he saw Abood and Rina raising their hands in surrender. Instead of taking them as captives, the hooligans made them face the wall. Then he saw one of the gang member shot Abood in his head. He fell to the ground followed by Rina. Omar became rooted and speechless, witnessing the man who had helped him raised his family, being killed brutally. Terrified of facing the same fate, he returned to the room. The children were awake because of the chaos outside. He asked them to stay quiet and stay put, otherwise the gangs would hear and kill all of them. The children were crying and Juliana tried her best to soothe them despite the tears of fear in her eyes. Falastin couldn't contained herself any longer. She wanted to pee so badly so she moved quietly to the toilet outside the house.

Some members of the gangs came toward Omar's family home. One of them jumped on the wall and he saw all the family gathered in the same room. He informed other members about them. They prepared the explosives and quietly placed them around the house. Soon after turned away, the house exploded. They brought the bulldozer and demolished the remains. Darkness enveloped the area and stillness hovered over the place after they left.

As soon as the morning light has broken, upon hearing that the gangs had left, the villagers who fled before, decided to return back to see what happened. Their houses were reduced to rubble and their field burnt down. Several dead villagers lay on the streets, sinking in their blood. Several others were found hugging each other, also in pool of blood.

They moved to Omar's house to find it destroyed too. Knowing all of his family were inside, they started screaming to the other villagers to help remove the rubble. Someone could be alive beyond all that. While doing so, they heard a faint voice asking for help. The neighbours quickly removed the debris to find out Falastin alive. They continued digging through to find if any of her family was as lucky as she was. Unfortunately, several metres away from the place they found Falastin, the rest of the family were cuddling together, dead.

Falastin, the sole survivor in Omar's family embrace her parents' spirit in loving her country, Palestine. She intends to continue her father's dream no matter what happens in the future.

Made in the USA
Las Vegas, NV
31 March 2022

46610721R00049